Power Plays

Power Plays

Collin Wilcox

Random House: New York

All rights reserved under International and Pan-American Copyright
Conventions. Published in the United States by Random House, Inc., New
York, and simultaneously in Canada by Random House of Canada Limited,
Toronto.

Library of Congress Cataloging in Publication Data
Wilcox, Collin.
Power plays.
I. Title.
PZ4.W665Po 1979 [PS3573.I395] 813'.5'4 78-23749
ISBN O-394-50172-1

Manufactured in the United State of America
9 8 7 6 5 4 3 2
First Edition

This book is dedicated to
Lurton Blassingame,
a gentleman

Power Plays

One

I was sitting at the head of the table; Ann was sitting at the foot. Ann's two sons, Billy and Dan, sat on either side. The occasion was a small celebration. A grammar-school teacher, Ann had just learned that tomorrow a TV crew would film her fourth-graders as they painted a mural on a playground wall. So we were celebrating with a rack of lamb for Ann, spaghetti for Billy, macaroni and cheese for Dan and pound cake for me. It was a family-style scene, evoking family-style memories, and during the meal I'd constantly found my thoughts wandering back into the past—the distant past and the recent past. I'd been divorced for more than ten years; Ann had been divorced for two years. I'd met her a little less than a year ago when Dan, her teen-age son, had been a witness to murder— briefly a suspect. I'd been looking for Dan when I'd first seen Ann. I'd been standing on her front porch when she'd opened the door. In my left hand I'd held my badge. My right hand had been free, ready to draw my revolver. Teen-agers, I'd learned, could be dangerous.

When Ann saw the badge she'd taken a quick, involuntary step backward, at the same time raising one hand to her mouth in the classic gesture of a woman distressed. She'd been wearing blue jeans and an old turtleneck sweater. Her thick, tawny hair had been loose around her shoulders. Her feet had been bare: five toes with pink-painted toenails peeping from beneath denims that dragged on the floor. Her eyes had been wide, mutely searching mine.

Even in that first moment I'd sensed something unique about her—something special, for me. Without her shoes, dressed in her old sweater and faded jeans, she'd seemed very vulnerable: a small, slim woman, deeply troubled. In her hushed, wide-eyed anxiety for her child, she'd seemed especially feminine, especially appealing. Looking down at her toes, I'd decided that she was slightly pigeon-toed. Later, I discovered that I'd been wrong.

Now, dressed in a beige silk blouse that accented her hair, sitting at the foot of a polished pine table that had been in her family for three generations, Ann seemed very assured—and still very appealing. She reached for her wineglass, smiled at me and lifted the glass in a silent toast. As she drank, her gray eyes regarded me with grave good humor. About the time I discovered that she wasn't pigeon-toed, I also discovered the intriguing difference between Ann's public and private personalities. With strangers she was often remote, reserved. With her friends, though, she shared a private warmth and quiet sense of pixy-lit humor.

Making love, she could be bold—playfully bawdy, even.

Noisily swallowing a huge bite of lamb, Billy turned to me. At age eleven he was a quick-thinking, quick-talking extrovert with a lively imagination and a vivid sense of himself.

"When I'm sixteen," he announced, "I'm going to learn how to fly an airplane. That's all you have to be—just sixteen. Then, after I get out of college, I'm going to be an aeronautical engineer. They design airplanes."

4

"Oh, God." Dan, seventeen, raised his eyes to the ceiling. "Last week he was going to be a scuba diver and discover sunken treasure. That was after he saw *The Deep*."

"And after *you* saw *The Deep*," Billy retorted, "you bought a poster of Jacqueline Bisset."

"In her T-shirt," Ann added, smiling mischievously. "Wet."

Suddenly flushing, Dan lowered his eyes to his plate. Frowning, he began to cut his meat busily. Whenever Ann mentioned sex, however obliquely, Dan quickly dropped out of the conversation. If she persisted, he'd leave the room. As Billy's high-pitched voice trilled in the background of my thoughts, I tried to recall whether I'd ever talked about sex with my mother. When I was thirteen my father had deserted us. He'd been a big, good-looking man with broad shoulders, bold eyes and an easy smile. As a young man he'd played semi-pro baseball. Later, after several unsuccessful big-league tryouts, he'd done "a little of everything." Finally settling down in San Francisco, he married my mother and began selling real estate. Eventually he opened his own real estate office. One day I'd come home to find my mother crying. Silently, she'd handed me a letter. My father had gone away with his secretary. He was sorry, he said. He couldn't help himself. He was taking the car, but nothing else. When he was settled, he'd send money.

Four years later he'd died in an auto accident in Texas. The car had caught fire, and he'd been burned beyond recognition. Except for the checks he mailed at Christmas, and sometimes on my birthday, he never sent us the money he'd promised.

In those four years my mother and I had never discussed sex. I was sure of it. I couldn't remember our talking of anything substantive. We almost never argued. But we never really talked, either. She'd been numbed by despair and loneliness. I'd been trying to find my way through adolescence—alone.

Obliquely, I glanced at Dan. What were his fantasies, contemplating Jacqueline Bisset in her wet T-shirt? Dan was a handsome boy, big for his age. He carried himself gracefully. His features were regular; his dark eyes were calm and clear. He was a quiet boy, slow to reveal either anger or pleasure. While Billy warbled, Dan watched.

"Are you ready for coffee, Frank?" Ann asked.

I shook my head. "I think I'll pass."

"Sanka?"

"No. Nothing."

"We've got some Ovaltine," Billy said. "How about some Ovaltine?"

I smiled at him. "Thanks, Billy. But—"

In the hallway close by, a telephone rang. Dan quickly rose from the table and answered the phone. During dinner he'd already taken two calls. Both the callers, I'd guessed, had been girls.

"It's for you, Frank," he called. "Inspector Canelli."

Resigned, I dropped my napkin beside my plate and pushed back my chair. I alternated "on call" nights with Pete Friedman, my co-lieutenant in Homicide. Tonight was my turn.

I waited for Dan to return to the dining room before I answered the phone.

"Lieutenant Hastings?" Canelli asked.

"Yes. What is it, Canelli?" As I spoke, I took a notebook and pen from my jacket pocket.

"Well, Lieutenant," Canelli said heavily, "I hate to bother you. But I've got a real situation here, it looks like. And I gotta have some authorizations."

"What's the situation?"

"The situation is that there was this traffic accident at Columbus and Vallejo. It was a fender bender, no big deal. A woman driving a silver-colored Mercedes hit a couple of guys in a brown Buick. She ran a red light and hit them in

6

the right front fender. But then, Jesus, it all hit the fan. Because the two guys in the Buick—the driver and another guy in back—they suddenly jumped out of the car and started to run. Well—" He paused for breath. Canelli had his own long-winded, rambling style, making a report. No matter how tight the time frame, he built the suspense. "Well, Columbus is pretty heavily traveled, as you well know. And there just happened to be a two-man black-and-white unit going north on Columbus that saw the whole thing. When they see the two guys running away from the Buick, one of the patrolmen from the unit took out after the driver. And his partner, he secured the accident scene. So then—" Again, he paused for breath.

"Listen, Canelli. Get to the point, will you? I haven't had dessert yet."

"Oh. Yeah. Sorry, Lieutenant. Well, the goddamn point is that it turns out there was another guy in the Buick. He was in the back seat. And he's dead."

I sighed. From where I stood I could look into the dining room. Billy was serving the dessert: chilled fruit cocktail with a slice of pound cake on the side. Anticipating the dessert, I'd only had one small helping of the rack of lamb.

"Go on, Canelli," I said heavily. "What's the rest of it?"

"Well, Lieutenant, I just got here. I haven't been here for more than five minutes. So I'm flying blind, you might say. But to me it looks like the guy was either shot or stabbed. But that's not the problem."

"What's the problem, Canelli?"

"The problem is the goddamn traffic, Lieutenant. It's backed up all the way down to Market Street. There's two sergeants from Traffic here. Ferguson and Durrant. And they're raising hell. They want me to move the car. But I've told them that I can't move the body without authorization. So *they* claim that all I'm moving is the car, not the body. So that's why I'm calling, Lieutenant. For instructions."

"You tell Ferguson and Durrant on my authority that the cars aren't to be moved. Tell them they've got to set up a permanent traffic diversion."

"Okay, Lieutenant." It was a doubtful-sounding rejoinder.

"Make them swallow it, Canelli," I said. "If the victim was shot, the shot could've come from outside the car. If we move the car, we lose our angle of fire."

"Yeah. Okay." Still doubtfully.

"What about the two men from the Buick? Did they get away?"

"One of them—the guy that was sitting in back—he got away. But the driver, he might be cornered. Like I said, one of the patrolmen took out after him and saw him duck into an alleyway that runs beside a three-story building. So the patrolman called for a backup, instead of going after him alone. Which was the right thing to do, of course. But then, when the backup arrived, and they swept the alleyway, they didn't get the guy."

"What does the patrolman think?"

"He thinks the guy's hiding in the building. There was a window broken, so I guess he's probably right."

"Have you got the building sewed up?"

"Yes, sir. Sewed up tight." He hesitated, then said, "Are you going to come down, Lieutenant?"

Reluctantly, I nodded. "I'll be there in about ten minutes, Canelli. Just keep the lid on until I get there. Don't move the cars. Don't go in after the suspect. Don't do anything except make the calls to the coroner and the lab. Just keep it cool."

"Right. Thanks, Lieutenant. Thanks a lot."

"You're welcome." I stepped into the dining room, kissed Ann, apologized, and reached across the table for my slice of pound cake. I'd eat it while I drove.

Two

With my siren wailing and my red light flashing, I drove the final two blocks on Vallejo Street against an angry, wildly weaving flow of one-way traffic. Ahead, I could see the Columbus-Vallejo intersection. Canelli hadn't exaggerated. With emergency lights winking from roofs and windshields, a half-dozen official vehicles blocked three of the four traffic lanes on Columbus Avenue. I parked beside a fire hydrant, left my card on the dashboard and locked my car. As I walked the last half block, I pinned my badge on the lapel of my corduroy sports jacket. The night was soft and warm, unusual for November. Overhead, stars sparkled in a dark, clear sky. If there was fog tonight, it lay west of the Golden Gate, miles from the city.

Columbus Avenue passes through the oldest, most historic section of downtown San Francisco. Carrying two-way traffic, Columbus begins among the towering skyscrapers of the city's financial district, touches the bawdy glitter of the old Barbary Coast and ends at Fisherman's Wharf. The Vallejo intersection is about halfway between the financial district and Broadway, center of the skin trade. On Vallejo Street, most of the buildings are old, built of brick and stone. Many of the buildings had survived the 1906 earthquake.

As I ducked under a makeshift rope barricade loosely strung between two lamp poles, I saw Canelli step from behind a coroner's van and walk quickly toward me. At age twenty-seven—at a suety, shapeless two hundred forty pounds—Canelli looked more like an overweight fry cook than a homicide detective. When he walked, he waddled. When he was worried, he perspired. Now, in the glare of police department floodlights, his broad, swarthy face glistened with sweat.

As Canelli approached me from the left, Traffic Sergeant Ferguson came at me from the right. We converged close to the brown Buick sedan. The car was angled across an inside lane of Columbus, headed north. The silver Mercedes had evidently come west on Vallejo, crashing into the Buick's right front fender and grill. The position of the cars made it impossible for either the Mercedes or the Buick to be driven forward.

Both cars were four-door sedans. On the driver's side of the Buick, the front door was standing slightly ajar. On the opposite side, a rear door stood wide open. Ignoring Canelli and Ferguson, I stepped to the open rear door, crouched and looked inside. A five-hundred-watt floodlight had been set up to shine through the open door. In the glare I saw the body of a man propped in the far corner of the rear seat.

He was wearing gray woolen slacks, a thigh-length brown car coat and a lemon-colored turtleneck sweater. His brown loafers were brightly shined; his expensive clothing was neatly pressed. His head lolled back against the seat cushions. From where I stood I could only see his throat, the underside of his chin and his foreshortened face. His thick-growing hair was gray, modishly long. The flesh of his neck and jowls was flaccid, middle-age slack. He'd worn a tweed hat that was now jammed between his head and the cloth headliner of the car. His coat was double-breasted, with leather buttons and leather trim at the collar and cuffs. The coat was unbuttoned, open across his chest. Above his heart, the ribbed, yellow material of his shirt was stained by a small circle of blood, hardly larger than a half dollar. The blood was red, still wet. The area around the stain was smudged, as if someone had tried to rub the stain—or stop the bleeding. His left arm was close to his side, pinioned against the car door. His left hand lay in his lap, palm up. His right arm was flung away from his body, lying across the seat cushions. The fingers of both hands were crooked in death's final claw of agony. On his left hand he wore a gold signet ring. The hands were long and thin, crisscrossed by blue veins. Like the neck and jowls, the texture of the hands suggested a man in his fifties or sixties.

Careful not to touch the car with my hands, I leaned forward through the open door until I could reach his right hand, lying on the seat. The flesh was still warm. Clammy, but still warm. He probably hadn't been dead for more than an hour.

Still crouching, I minutely examined the interior of the car, and the seat cushions. I saw nothing—no spattered blood, no bits of discarded paper, no cigarette butts or burned matches or other refuse. My shadow lay across his legs, obscuring the floor of the car. Stepping aside and squatting on my heels, I looked carefully at the richly carpeted floor. I saw an ice pick lying between the victim's polished brown loafers. It was a professional-style pick, with a solid metal handle. The pick's tine was bloody, but the handle was unstained, doubtless wiped clean of both blood and fingerprints. Behind the victim's left foot, between the loafer and the door, I caught a glimpse of a torn scrap of wax paper.

Knees cracking, I straightened and half turned to Canelli. "What's that?" I asked, pointing to the scrap of wax paper.

"I'm not sure," he answered. "I didn't want to move it until you got here."

I took out my ball-point pen, leaned into the car and used the pen to push the fragment of paper away from the victim's foot. A larger piece of paper was attached to the fragment. Both torn pieces, fitted together and flattened, formed an envelope measuring about eight inches square. "Compress, 6 x 6 Inches" was printed in blue block letters on the envelope. I returned the fragments to their original position and backed out of the car without touching anything but the carpeting.

"It's the wrapping from a surgical pad," I said. I pointed to the small circle of still-wet blood in the center of the yellow turtleneck shirt. "He was probably stabbed with the pick, and then a compress was used to soak up the blood. That's the reason for those smudges around the wound."

"I'll be damned," Canelli said, surprised. Then, marveling, "That's planning."

"Is there anything else? Anything I missed?"

"There's a big lump over his right temple. You can see it through the rear window."

"Was the skin broken?" I asked.

"No, sir."

I nodded thoughtfully, at the same time turning my attention to the front seat of the car. The mirror, I noticed, was angled so that the driver couldn't see into the rear seat. For the first time, I realized that the car's engine was still running—and the temperature gauge was glowing red. I took out my handkerchief and turned the ignition key, killing the engine. "Take this key to the lab," I ordered.

I looked carefully at the death scene one last time, then stepped away from the car. Ferguson, the traffic sergeant, stepped forward. Ferguson was an old-timer—a motorcycle cop who still preferred two-wheelers to a squad car. Wearing a white helmet, dressed in a bulky double-breasted black jacket, with a big .44 Magnum swinging on his hip, he looked like a storm trooper.

"When can we move the car, Lieutenant?" His voice was thick and hoarse, roughened by years of riding in the wind. "I got traffic backed up for two miles." As he spoke, he turned to face me squarely, gauntleted hands propped pugnaciously on his hips, fists clenched. His booted legs were spread wide apart.

"First," I said, pointing to the body, "I've got to have pictures and prints and measurements." I nodded to three lab technicians and a photographer standing close by, each carrying the tools of his trade. "And also," I said, "we've got to see if we can find that driver."

Beneath the visor of his helmet, Ferguson was scowling at me. I turned to Canelli. "Where's the suspect? Which building?"

Canelli pointed north on Columbus, toward Broadway's pornographic neon glare. Half a block away, two patrol cars were parked in front of a brownstone building. Three patrolmen stood in front of an alleyway that opened on the north side of the brownstone. A six-foot ornamental iron gate secured the alleyway. Since the building was attached to its neighbor on both sides, the gate offered the only outside access to the rear of the building. The gate was standing open. As I watched, a technician was setting up a floodlight in front of the open gate. A long electrical line snaked across Columbus to a portable generator placed on the opposite sidewalk. I saw the technician attach the line to the floodlight and throw a switch. The empty alleyway was bathed in bright white light.

"One of those patrolmen from the black-and-white unit knows the terrain, Lieutenant," Canelli was saying. "His name's Hunsinger. Or Hunsicker. Something like that. Anyhow, he's the one I told you about—the one that chased the driver. You want me to come with you?"

Instead of replying, I took a moment to survey the scene.

In the glare of the floodlight, amid the confusion of electrical cables and cordoned-off spectators and the impersonal metallic blare of police radios, we might have been on a Hollywood set. "Is anyone else here from Homicide?" I asked.

"No, sir."

"Then you stay here. Make sure the technicians don't screw up when they go over the Buick. Especially be careful of that compress wrapping. It'll take good prints. Be sure it's photographed. Then you—personally—put it in a plastic bag, and take it downtown for printing. Don't let them print it here. It looks like the handle of the pick's been wiped. And maybe the door's been wiped, too. But he might've forgotten that wrapping. Clear?"

"Yes, sir." Canelli nodded. "That's clear."

I turned to Ferguson, at the same time glancing pointedly down at the nonregulation Magnum slung low on his hip. Ferguson was a tough-talking, tough-acting cop—at least in the squad room.

"Let's go take a look, Ferguson," I said. "Let's see if we can find him."

As I turned toward the building, I thought I saw Ferguson's habitual scowl give way to a blink of uncertainty.

"Are you Hunsinger" I asked a tall, loose-limbed officer with a narrow, unformed face and a fierce-looking gunfighter's mustache. He couldn't have been more than twenty-two years old.

"That's, ah, 'Hunsicker,' sir," he said. "With a 'k.' " His Adam's apple bobbed apologetically.

"What's the situation?" I asked, turning to stare into the alleyway. "Fill me in."

"Well, ah—" Hunsicker edged toward the alleyway, at the same time awkwardly gesturing for me to precede him. "Well, we were coming south on Columbus, and we saw the accident. I was driving. So I pulled over to the curb.

14

Just about then, the driver jumped out of the Buick and started running. I told my partner to check out the accident, for injuries." He paused, tentatively looking at me.

I nodded approval. "You did right. What happened next?"

Hunsicker pointed back toward the scene of the accident. "The driver crossed in front of that bookstore—" His long, bony forefinger traced the route of flight. "Then he turned in this direction. I called for him to halt, but he just ran faster. This gate was half open. When he came to it, he dodged inside. I know these buildings along here. I know how they're laid out, and I figured he was trapped. So I laid back, waiting for my partner." Again he looked hesitantly at me; again I nodded approval.

"But when my partner got here," Hunsicker continued, "he told me about the body. So we agreed that, first of all, we had to secure the accident scene. For evidence."

"Good. I'm glad you did. Can you describe the suspect?" As I spoke, I studied the alleyway. On the right, a sheer concrete wall rose three stories high. On the left, I saw a doorway and three windows, all unbarred. Fragments of broken glass sparkled on the pavement beneath the third window.

"He's medium height, medium build," Hunsicker answered. "He ran like a young man. Dark hair, no hat. He was wearing dark pants and a light-colored jacket. It was short, like a windbreaker."

"Did you see his face?"

"No, sir," he answered regretfully. "Sorry, but I didn't."

"Did he show a weapon?"

"No. He just ran. He only looked over his shoulder once, when I first challenged him."

I stepped back for a better view of the building. The ground floor was a lighted storefront displaying leather clothing, boots and accessories. Above the display windows

I saw two floors of dark, empty loft windows under a sign that read "Anderson's Theatricals."

"They make theater props," Hunsicker offered. "Scenery, things like that."

"Is the back covered?"

"Yes, sir. But I don't think he got out that way. I don't think he had time. He had to've gone inside the building, through that window. From there—from inside the building—the only way out is by a fire escape. I knew that, so as soon as I got here and saw that broken window, I climbed up on that fence, there—" He pointed to an eight-foot fence blocking the end of the alleyway. For the first time I saw a uniformed man sitting on top of the fence. He was idly swinging his feet, like a boy dangling his legs over a riverbank. In his arms he cradled a shotgun. "That way, I could see both the fire escape and the side door," Hunsicker said. "Except for the front door, through the store, there's no other way out."

"So you think he's still in there."

"Yes, sir," he answered firmly. "Yes, sir, I think he's still in there."

"Where does that side door lead?"

"To the storeroom in back of The Latigo. That's the name of the store. But there's also an inside stairway that leads up to Anderson's."

"Have you ever been inside this building?"

"Yes, sir, I have. Several times. Until a few months ago, this was my beat on foot patrol. And, ah.— He cleared his throat and shifted to a stiffer stance. "I, ah, knew a girl who worked at Anderson's."

While we'd been talking, two other uniformed men had arrived, both carrying shotguns. Counting the man on top of the fence, I had seven men on the scene.

I turned to the two new arrivals. "You two men cover the front, here—the door of The Latigo. You two—" I gestured to another pair of patrolmen, strangers to me. "You stay in the alleyway here for backup. The three of us

16

will go inside." I took a moment to coordinate walkie-talkie channels, and ordered Hunsicker to take one of the shotguns. Then I waved the four men to their posts.

As they dispersed I turned to face Ferguson and Hunsicker. "I'll go in first," I said. "Hunsicker, you come next. Then you, Ferguson." I turned away and walked into the alleyway, stopping before the broken window. On the pavement beneath the window, among the shards of broken glass, I saw a length of splintered broomstick. He'd used the broomstick to break out the glass.

I cupped my hands to my mouth and shouted through the gaping window: "All right, this is the police. The building's surrounded. I want you to come out of there. Come out through the window, the way you went in. But before you do it, sing out. Tell us you're coming. Otherwise, we'll blow your head off."

No response.

"You've got ten seconds," I called. "Ten seconds, starting right now."

Methodically, I counted off the seconds while I fruitlessly strained to hear some sound of movement from inside. With the time counted out, I whispered over my shoulder, "Have you both got flashlights?"

Yes, they did.

"Okay, here we go," I said, still whispering. "Take it slow and easy. When you're inside, get out of line with the window."

As I pulled myself up on the window sill and dropped to the floor inside the darkened storeroom, I was thankful that I'd worn casual clothes, eating dinner at Ann's. Over the years I'd torn too many suits in too many dark, unfamiliar rooms.

Drawing my revolver, I stepped cautiously to my left, away from the window. Holding the shotgun in one hand, Hunsicker followed immediately, landing light on his feet. Ferguson was next, awkward and noisy, dropping to the floor with a board-rattling crash.

17

"Stay here," I ordered. "I'll find a light switch." With my eyes growing accustomed to the dim light from the window, I made my way between rows of stacked packing cases to an inside door. I found the switch, alerted the two officers, and turned on the overhead lights. While I stood motionless, Ferguson and Hunsicker searched the storeroom, unsuccessfully. I checked the door to The Latigo's showroom. It was securely locked from the inside.

"Here, Lieutenant." It was Hunsicker's voice. "Here's where he went."

I found Hunsicker standing before a short flight of stairs that led to an old-fashioned glass-paned door marked "Anderson's Theatricals." The door was closed, but the small pane closest to the doorknob had been broken out.

"I'll go up first," I said, eyeing the two patrolmen. "Don't bunch up behind me on the stairs, in case something happens. When we get up there, let's spread out. Clear?"

In unison, the two men nodded. Hunsicker's eyes were steady, meeting mine squarely. But second by second Ferguson was looking less ferocious. He was unable to meet my eyes—unable to keep himself from repeatedly swallowing.

I pointed to Hunsicker's shotgun. "Have you got a round in the chamber?" I asked.

"No, sir." Properly, he'd waited for orders.

"Do it."

He jacked a shell into the chamber, then eased down the hammer. I nodded. I didn't want him behind me with the gun's hammer raised. At close range, a round of twelve-gauge buckshot would take off my leg. I would take a chance on the extra second it would take him to cock the gun and fire.

"All right," I said. "Let's do it." I shifted my revolver to my left hand and used my right hand to reach cautiously through the broken-out pane and turn the doorknob from the inside. Then, standing aside, I pushed the door slowly open. Backlight from the storeroom illuminated the first few stairs of a longer flight that ended in darkness on the floor above. I saw a light switch just inside the door. Motioning for the two patrolmen to stand back, I flicked on the light at the top of the stairs.

Instantly, a shot crashed.

Then another.

The light exploded, showering incandescent fragments down on the stairs before us.

In a sudden, desperate confusion of guns and awkward limbs and incoherent obscenities, each of us found cover.

"God—*damn.*" It was Ferguson, blustering. "Goddamn son of a bitch." Looking at him, I saw the six-inch barrel of the Magnum trembling. The gun's hammer was drawn back, ready to fire.

"Lower that hammer," I breathed.

Momentarily, he blinked at the fury in my voice before he looked down at the gun. Then, with the muzzle pointed at the ceiling, he lowered the hammer.

As I reached for Hunsicker's walkie-talkie, I looked again into the young patrolman's eyes. His answering gaze was still steady and calm.

"Bring some tear gas and a launcher to the alleyway window," I ordered, speaking softly into the walkie-talkie. "And three gas masks. *Now.*"

On the walkie-talkie, a disembodied voice acknowledged the order.

"You take them through the window, Ferguson," I ordered, "and holster your goddamn weapon."

Muttering, he rose from his crouched position and wheeled away, angrily thrusting the Magnum into his hog-leg holster as he stalked toward the open window. I was standing close beside the open door, protected by a narrow angle of the wall. Hunsicker was in a similar position on the other side of the doorway. I watched him take off his hat and put it carefully on a packing case. Without the hat, Hunsicker looked even younger, more vulnerable. His sandy hair grew in cowlicks, like a boy's.

"Give me the shotgun," I whispered, holstering my revolver. "You shoot the gas."

Silently, he handed over the shotgun. At the same time he stole a quick glance up the darkened stairs. From above, I thought I caught the sound of floorboards creaking. At the same moment I heard a familiar voice from behind me: "*Psst.* Lieutenant. Want me to come inside?" Holding a grenade launcher, Canelli stood in the open window. Seeing the familiar face, I was conscious of an irrational, knee-weakened rush of relief.

"Come in," I whispered. "Bring the equipment. Leave Ferguson outside." Then, as Canelli began clambering through the window, I stopped him.

"Tell Ferguson to put two men directly under the fire escape."

Relaying the order, Canelli finally managed to struggle through the window with the tear-gas paraphernalia. Moments later, with the gas masks covering our faces, we were ready.

"Here goes the gas," I said, speaking softly into the radio. "Is that fire escape double-covered?"

"It's covered." I recognized the rasp of Ferguson's voice.

I put the walkie-talkie carefully on a lower step, then looked at Canelli. "Ready?" My voice was a stranger's, muffled by the gas mask.

Pressing his outsized body against a sidewall, Canelli stood with his revolver crossed over his chest. Behind the goggle-round lenses of the gas mask, his soft brown eyes evoked the irrational image of a benevolent space visitor. Slowly he nodded. I turned to Hunsicker, asking the same question. He cocked the grenade launcher, released the safety catch and nodded. Beneath the gas mask his Adam's apple move convulsively.

"All right," I said. "Do it."

Quickly, Hunsicker ducked around the door frame, fired the grenade, than ducked back to safety. On the floor above, the grenade popped. A moment later I heard the angry hiss of C.S. gas.

"Again."

Quickly, Hunsicker reloaded the launcher and fired. His movements were quick and sure.

"That's enough," I said. "Let's—"

From upstairs I heard the sudden sound of violent coughing.

"We got him." As I spoke, I stepped into the open doorway, holding the shotgun ready. Yellowish clouds of gas were billowing out of the darkness at the top of the stairs. The coughing was sharper now—but seemed to come from farther away. Footsteps rattled on bare wooden floors; something crashed to the floor, toppled by the blinded man above. The sounds came from my right, toward the back of the building. I realized that I was perspiring heavily. Inside my gas mask, the plastic eyepieces were fogging over. Beneath my mask, the gas combined with perspiration, stinging my neck. Belatedly, I realized that I should have buttoned my collar.

"Throw the gun down," I shouted. "I want to hear it hit the floor. Then we'll take you out."

Two shots roared, followed in a few seconds by a crash of glass. A moment later Ferguson's voice came from the walkie-talkie: "He's thrown something through the window, back here. A chair. The window's on the fire escape."

I picked up the walkie-talkie. "You'd better take cover, Ferguson. Don't take any chances."

"Don't worry." Even through the soft sizzle of the walkie-talkie's static, I could hear the fervor in his voice. Suddenly I realized that in all his years on the force, Ferguson had never faced a gun.

I replaced the radio and turned again to the stairway. "I'm going up. Canelli, you come behind me. Hunsicker,

21

you come next. When we get to the top of the stairs, I want you on my right, Canelli. You're on my left, Hunsicker. Clear?"

Silently, impassively, the two masked figures nodded in unison.

Slowly, cautiously, I began climbing the stairs. As I came closer to the top, the eddying gas swirled around me like deadly yellow fog. The pain at my neck became almost unbearable. Through the sweat-fogged lenses of my gas mask, only a small circle in the center was clear. My hands and wrists began to sting.

At the top of the stairs, bending double, I turned toward a row of windows at the rear of the building: five tall rectangles, pale in the yellow-misted darkness.

In front of the center window I saw a ghostly silhouette: a man's head and shoulders.

"I see him," I whispered over my shoulder. "Hold it. Stay back." I drew back the shotgun's hammer, fitted its stock to my shoulder and fired at the window above the shadowy head. Through the musical tinkle of falling glass, I heard a scream.

"*Jesus. Don't. I quit.*" I heard a heavy metallic thud. "There's the gun. Take the goddamn gun."

I jacked another shell into the chamber and left the hammer cocked. Through the fogged-over lenses of my mask, I could hardly make him out. "Walk toward me. Walk toward the sound of my voice. Put your hands on your head."

"Christ—" He was snuffling, beginning to blubber: "Christ, I'm cut by the glass. I'm hurt."

"If you don't come toward me with your hands on your head, right now—right this second—you'll be dead."

Stumbling, sniffling, coughing, he was finally obeying.

Three

With a suspect in custody, my next concern was concluding the on-site investigation, assuring the vital chain of evidence that must hold from the moment the crime is discovered until the jury brings in a verdict. I ordered Canelli to take the suspect downtown while I supervised the investigation's final phase: a witnessed, signed-and-countersigned confiscation of the victim's personal effects, followed by the authorized removal of the body.

By one-thirty in the morning, traffic on Columbus Avenue had returned to normal.

I was tempted to call Canelli at headquarters, telling him that I'd interrogate the suspect in the morning. Finally, though, curiosity overcame fatigue. From an examination of the victim's effects, I'd learned that his name had probably been Eliot Murdock. He'd probably lived in Los Angeles. He'd probably been staying at the Beresford Hotel, in San Francisco. Judging by his clothing and general grooming, he'd probably been a respected citizen.

I was curious to know who had killed him—and why.

Canelli was in the interrogation room. Before joining the

23

interrogation, I stepped into a darkened anteroom, where I could watch the suspect through a two-way mirror. The suspect was sitting at a small steel table, facing the mirror. Hands in his pockets, Canelli leaned against the far wall, morosely studying the suspect. A patrolman assigned to interrogation security stood beside the room's small metal door. The patrolman carried neither a gun, nor cuffs, nor a nightstick. But his shoulders were big and beefy, and he wore thick leather gloves with small strips of steel sewn into each finger.

The suspect looked about thirty years old. He was wearing dark slacks and a tan poplin windbreaker, just as Hunsicker had described him. His dark hair was thinning on top. He appeared to weigh about a hundred sixty pounds. His face was pale and thin; his nose was too long, his chin too sharp. His mouth was narrow and unformed: a childlike mouth, with the upper lip protruding over the lower lip. Beneath eyebrows that almost met, his brown eyes were dull and muddy. His hair was medium long. Where the glass had cut him, fresh bandages covered the left half of his forehead and the back of his left hand.

Now Canelli began talking. Without appearing to listen, the suspect moved his eyes constantly around the small interrogation room, as if he were looking for a way out. I reached to the right of the mirror and switched on a small loudspeaker.

". . . don't seem to realize the spot you're in, Dick." Canelli was speaking in an elaborately reasonable voice, pretending a big-brother's concern for the suspect. "I mean, you claim you were bum rapped. And it seems to me that you mean it—that you're telling me the truth. But Jesus, Dick, you got to put yourself in my position. I'm willing to help you, if I can. I'm willing to go out on a limb for you, with the lieutenant. But before I do that, you gotta help me. You been around long enough to know how it goes. And you—"

"But I *told* you," the suspect broke in. "I told you how it came down. I told you *everything*. There's nothing more to *tell* you." His voice was high and shrill: a thin, plaintive bleat. His long-fingered, big-knuckled hands rapidly clenched and unclenched on the metal table before him. As he spoke he looked straight into the mirror, as if he were beseeching me to help him. I saw fear in his eyes. But I saw caution, too—and calculation. He'd been arrested before. He knew the moves.

"You told me how it went," Canelli said, "but I gotta have names. Before I can help you, I gotta have names."

"But I don't *have* no names. Christ, I already told you how it happened. I told you everything—every single thing. I got nothing more to tell you."

Sighing regretfully, Canelli dolefully shook his head. "If that's true, Dick, then it's your ass. I mean, right there we've got enough for murder one, no question. But then, Jesus, you try to kill us, in that goddamn loft. And you—"

"But I *didn't*. I just—Christ—I just shot at the light. I just wanted *out*. Christ, I—I was scared. I already *told* you. I—Jesus—suddenly I see a goddamn stiff, in the back seat. So I start running. What would you've done?"

"I'm not talking about running, Dick," Canelli said softly. "I'm talking about shooting. And you shot at us four times. I was there. I know. I was counting." Again, Canelli sadly shook his head. In his wrinkled, shapeless suit, head hanging and shoulders slumped, Canelli was deep in the role of the suspect's anxious, helpless friend. It was a part Canelli could play to perfection. With his broad, earnest face, his guileless eyes and his roly-poly body, Canelli didn't look like a cop. He didn't act like a cop, either. In all his life, he'd told me once, he'd never hit a man in anger. I'd never seen him lose his temper, never heard him raise his voice. He was the only cop I'd ever known who could get his feelings hurt. Yet, facing danger—even death—Canelli was calm. A squad-room comic had once remarked that Canelli ducked so late that he got decorated for it.

". . . bum rapped, like you said," Dick was saying. "Christ, don't you know the truth when you hear it?"

Canelli shrugged. "The problem is, Dick, you gotta worry about the lieutenant. I believe what you're saying. I already told you that. But the lieutenant, that's something else. All he cares about are the facts. And the fact is that you were driving a car with a body in back. And you—"

"But it was the *other* guy. The guy in back. He's the one that did it. Christ, how'm I going to stab someone while I'm driving? How'm I going to *do* it?"

"I believe you," Canelli said soothingly. "I really do. But what I don't believe is that the guy in back—both guys— were strangers to you. I mean, you say that you were walking down Mason Street when some guy steps up to you and says he wants you to drive for him. He gives you fifty bucks, no questions asked. Then he tells you to drive to the Beresford Hotel, you say, and wait for him at the curb. He says he wants to pick up a friend, you claim. And he does pick up a friend. And then—"

"And then they get in the back seat." Now the suspect was perspiring heavily, wiping at his glistening forehead with an unsteady hand. He began blinking rapidly, as if blinded by a bright light. Looking into his eyes, I thought I could see the drug addict's pinpointed pupils. "Both of them, they got in the back together. And the guy—the one that hired me—he tells me to drive out Bush Street, and then go left on Kearny, and then left again on Columbus. He tells me to drive slow. He tells me to turn the radio up, loud. And turn up the mirror, too, he says. And I did. So then, Christ, this broad hit us. And the next thing I know, the guy's telling me to split—to run. The other guy's dead, he says. So I look and, Jesus, the guy *is* dead. So I ran. I was scared, and I ran. And—" Wiping his streaming face with a trembling hand, he looked at Canelli with hollow eyes. "Listen, can I have a glass of water, or something?"

Canelli nodded sympathetically. "Sure, Dick. Sure you can. But first give it to me again—the description of the guy who gave you the fifty."

The suspect sighed: a ragged, noisy exhalation. He was almost used up, pushed to the edge. Suddenly he'd lost hope, lost his nerve. Without raising his voice—without taking his hands out of his pockets—Canelli had beaten him. "Jesus, I already *told* you."

"Tell me again," Canelli said gently. "Tell me one last time."

"He was—" The suspect tried to clear his throat, then coughed, then gulped down the phlegm. "He was in his thirties, I guess. I think he was blond, or sandy-haired. He was wearing a hat, so it was hard to tell. He was about my height—five ten—and maybe about my weight. He had on a topcoat and a hat—one of those cloth hats. He was a good dresser. Not fancy, but good. And he was a good talker, too."

"What'd you mean, a good talker?"

"I mean that he talked like—you know—he'd been to college, or something. Like that."

"How'd the other guy sound? The victim. Did he sound like he'd been to college, too?"

"I—I don't know. Honest. The other one, he told me to turn on the radio, like I said."

"And you didn't hear anything from the back seat, you claim. Nothing at all."

"Nothing. I swear to God."

Canelli nodded, thoughtfully studying the suspect. As the silence continued, I decided to push the button that illuminated a small red bulb over the door of the interrogation room. Canelli glanced at the light, glanced involuntarily at the two-way mirror and then pushed himself heavily away from the wall. "One glass of water," he said. "Coming up."

I stepped out into the hallway and walked with Canelli

to the end of the hallway. "You've got him going," I said. "Congratulations."

Canelli's broad, swarthy moon face broke into a smile. Canelli was always grateful for praise. "Thanks, Lieutenant. Thanks very much."

"What's his name? Has he got a record?"

Canelli took a notebook from his pocket. Licking his thumb, he frowned as he riffled the pages. Finally: "His name is Richard Blake. Age, thirty-two. Address, 387 Mason Street, in the Tenderloin. He's had convictions for pimping, drug dealing, grand-theft auto, breaking and entering and aggravated assault. He's on parole from Folsom for the assault charge, with four years to go."

"Who'd he assault?"

"A hooker. One of his girls, I guess."

"How do you figure his story?"

As he considered the question, Canelli yawned—excused himself, and yawned again. "To me," he said finally, "it sounds mostly like a straight story. Except that I don't buy the part about him not knowing the guy. I think he knows him. I figure maybe he's more scared of the guy than he is of a murder charge. For now, anyhow."

"Do you believe his account of what happened in the car?"

Canelli nodded—and yawned again. "Yes, sir, I guess I do. Excuse me."

"I believe him, too," I answered thoughtfully. "I think he's telling the truth. For one thing, the victim was registered at the Beresford. He had a room key in his pocket."

"That's good," Canelli said. "It's an intersecting point, as they say."

"What about the car?"

Once more licking his thumb, Canelli consulted the notebook. "It's registered to Walter Frazer, at 2710 Jackson Street. The car was reported stolen at twenty minutes after ten."

28

"Just a few minutes after the murder."

"Right."

"Has anyone talked to Walter Frazer?"

"No, sir. No one from Homicide, I mean. See, there was a stabbing out at Hunter's Point last night, and Marsten took it. And him and me, we were the only ones on duty last night. So I thought I'd wait to check with you before I got anyone out of bed." He looked at me anxiously—hoping for approval.

"It can wait until tomorrow. Who did talk to Walter Frazer?"

"The sector car took his report about eleven-thirty. Of course, they handled it like a routine stolen vehicle squeal."

I gestured to the door of the interrogation room. "What about him? Are you going to keep at him?"

"Well—" Canelli rubbed his dark-stubbled cheeks. "I was figuring that maybe I'd let him stew until morning. If I'm right—if he's not talking because he's scared—maybe he needs time to think it over. Besides, he's a junkie. I saw the needle marks. It's not much of a habit, by the marks. But, anyhow, it's a habit. So time's on our side."

"The route that he described—from the Beresford Hotel to Bush to Kearny to Columbus. Is he firm on that?"

"Yes, sir, he seems to be. I probably asked him five or six times. And I always got the same answer. Why?"

"I'm going to detail a couple of black-and-white cars to look for that compress," I answered. "It wasn't in the car, so I figure it was probably thrown out. It's a long shot, but it's worth an hour or two."

Canelli nodded agreement. "If we found it," he said, "it'd establish where the murder was probably committed."

I nodded agreement, thanked him for what he'd done, and walked down the hallway to the elevators. The time was two A.M. My eyes burned with fatigue, my legs felt rubbery, the muscles of my neck and shoulders ached. Rubbing my neck with one hand, I pushed the "down" button with the other. I found myself thinking about Eliot Murdock. He'd carried a hundred eighty dollars cash in his wallet, plus all the right credit cards, including American Express and the Diners Club. The quality of his clothing and the precision of his barbering and the pampered softness of his manicured hands all suggested someone with money to spend, places to go, people to see.

And someone had wanted him dead. Someone had planned his murder with skill and painstaking attention to detail.

Who? I wondered, stepping wearily into an empty elevator. And why?

Four

Promptly at nine the following morning I called Los Angeles Homicide and gave them the details of the case. I asked them to notify Murdock's next of kin and to arrange for positive identification. I also asked about the victim's address, 3636 Occidental Boulevard. Was it an affluent neighborhood? A quick poll taken in the Los Angeles squad room graded the neighborhood a "B."

By nine-thirty, documents on the case covered most of my desk: still-damp 8 x 10 glossies and a dozen-odd preliminary reports, most of them badly typed by sleepy policemen. All of the reports were Xerox copies. The originals were on their way through channels to R & I for filing.

By nine-forty-five, a secretary knocked on my door, entered, smiled at me and handed over a large manila folder neatly inscribed: *Murdock, Eliot ref AF-6143-478.* I thanked her, we exchanged smiles and I appreciatively watched the movement of her buttocks as she left my office. Dropping the folder into my "in" basket, I began studying the scattered pictures and reports, hoping to discover something new. I was disappointed. Even the medical examiner's report confirmed my first theory. The victim had been struck on the right temple with a "blackjacklike" weapon. The blow had resulted in a hairline fracture of the skull, and some inner cranial bleeding. But the fatal wound had been inflicted by an "ice-picklike" instrument that had "entered the chest cavity just beneath the sternum, continued at an upward angle and punctured the left ventricle of the heart." There had been only one puncture wound.

Conclusion: The murderer had either been very skillful or very lucky. Or both.

At five minutes to ten, I heard a familiar knock on my door. It was Pete Friedman, my senior co-lieutenant in Homicide. Friedman had served as lieutenant under Captain Kreiger while I'd advanced from detective second-grade to detective first-grade to detective sergeant. When Kreiger retired, a year ago, I'd been promoted to lieutenant—but Friedman hadn't made captain. Characteristically, he accepted his situation with a kind of wry, witty cynicism. Friedman was a first-rate detective—but a third-rate departmental politician.

Now, easing his bulging two hundred thirty pounds into my visitors' chair with a grateful sigh, Friedman pointed to the photographs. "Compared to the ones they got at Hunter's Point last night," he said, "those are pretty tame stuff."

"How do you know? You haven't seen these yet."

"I've seen the Hunter's Point pictures, though."

"And?"

"And apparently it was a lovers' triangle. The loser got castrated. First his throat was slit. Then he was castrated."

"Jesus. Really?"

Friedman nodded. "Really. The lady in question, when she saw the damage, picked up the knife and went looking for the winner, who, it happened, was her husband." He shook his head. "She wanted to show him how it felt, she said."

"Did she find him?"

"No." As he spoke he began unwrapping a cigar. It was

part of Friedman's daily ritual. Every morning, usually about ten o'clock, he came down the hallway, knocked on my door and settled himself into my visitors' chair. It was Friedman's contention that my visitors' chair was the only chair in the Department that really fitted him. Therefore, during the last year he'd devised various schemes for getting the chair into his office. Most of the schemes involved bets on football, all of which he'd lost. Altogether, the unsuccessful campaign had cost him more than fifty dollars.

After settling himself, Friedman began the lengthy process of lighting the day's first cigar. First he stripped off the cellophane wrapper, wadded it into a tight little ball and tossed it toward my wastepaper basket. Invariably, he missed the basket. Next he began the search for a match, grunting as he shifted his bulk from one big ham to the other, rummaging through his pockets. During the entire ritual he talked. Usually he talked about current homicide cases, airily theorizing on the particular case that most intrigued him. Some of his theories were fanciful, some were bizarre. In the end, though, most of them proved right. Over the years Friedman had developed an uncanny ability to guess the direction a homicide investigation would take.

Now, as I watched him, he'd finally located a match. The next part of the ceremony was inexorable. With the cigar finally lit, he sailed the match in a long, smoking arc toward my wastebasket. If the wrapper seldom found its mark, the match seldom missed.

"What about this—" He gestured again to the pages littering my desk. "What's the name? Murdock?"

"Right." I collected the pictures and handed them over—at the same time pointedly pushing an ashtray across the desk. It was, I knew, a pointless gesture. Most of Friedman's cigar ash landed first on his vest, then on my floor.

After riffling quickly through the pictures, Friedman returned to the picture we would use for identification. The picture had been carefully posed at the morgue and showed the victim with his hair combed, collar straightened, mouth closed and eyes open.

"You know," he said thoughtfully, "he looks familiar."

"Familiar? How?"

"I don't know—" Staring at the picture, Friedman drew on his cigar, then blew out the smoke in a slow, reflective curl. Physically, Friedman's face resembled Canelli's: broad and swarthy, with dark eyes and a full mouth. But their personalities were almost direct opposites—and so were the subtleties of their features. Canelli's soft brown eyes and large, mobile mouth registered everything he thought or felt, moment to moment. Friedman had sorcerer's eyes: lazy-lidded and shrewd—revealing nothing, seeing everything. When Friedman smiled, it was always at a very private joke. "What's his first name?" he asked, still studying the picture.

"Eliot."

"Eliot Murdock—" Suddenly he nodded decisively. The movement dislodged an inch-long cigar ash that dropped to his vest, than tumbled slow-motion to the floor. "Yeah. Eliot Murdock. He used to have a column. A syndicated column. He was even on TV for a while. That's how I remember the face. He was a commentator."

"A commentator?"

"Right. A political commentator. He did a kind of exposé thing. You know, like Jack Anderson. It was behind-closed-doors-in-Washington stuff. He was never a big-timer, though. I haven't heard anything about him for years. Ten, twelve years, at least."

"I didn't know you followed politics."

"I don't, I'm interested in politicians. Or, more to the point, I'm interested in con men. And nobody runs a con better than a politician."

I smiled. "You're a regular squad-room philosopher."

Friedman waved his cigar, burlesquing a gesture of self-depreciation. "An observer, let's say. A connoisseur." Another length of ash fell to the floor. Now the cigar waved in my direction, inviting me to continue. "What's the rundown?" he asked.

As concisely as I could, I gave him a chronological account of the Murdock homicide. As always, when I outlined a new case, Friedman sat perfectly still, eyes half closed, impassively smoking—a big-bellied Buddha in a wrinkled blue suit. When I finished the account, he nodded judiciously.

"I like it," he announced. "It's got a little of everything."

"Thank you." I tried to make it sound wry.

"What you've got to do is work on Richard Blake," Friedman advised. "If the murderer's a pro, he sure as hell didn't pick a stranger off Mason Street and give him fifty bucks to drive the murder car. By the way—" He paused, puffing on his cigar. "What about the owner of the Buick? What's he got to say?"

"I don't know," I admitted. "Canelli tried to get him at his home and his place of business this morning, but couldn't. He's still trying."

"It's possible that Blake stole the car. That's usually how it works. It's beneath a hit man's dignity to steal the car." As he spoke, Friedman levered himself forward in his chair, dropped his cigar stub in the ashtray and sank back with a sigh. "What about Murdock's luggage and clothing? Anything there?"

"To be honest," I said, "I haven't looked at them yet. They're still in Property. The technicians brought them in after they worked over Murdock's hotel room."

"You didn't look at his room yourself?" Mild disapproval was plain in the question.

"I thought Blake was more important," I said defensively. "The room will keep. As soon as I found Murdock's room key, I had the room sealed and guarded. After Canelli finds Walter Frazer, I'll have him and Marsten start work at the Beresford."

Friedman shook his head. "Not Marsten. He started at Hunter's Point. I want him to stay on it. Let's give Culligan to Canelli."

I nodded agreement, gave the orders to the squad room and called the holding cells, ordering Blake prepared for interrogation.

Five

I opened my leather badge case and banged the badge down hard on the small metal table. The table jumped. The suspect winced and turned his head away, as if to avoid a blow. But it was a sluggish, uncertain reaction. The suspect's head bobbed loosely. His eyes were dead, his mouth was slack.

Canelli had been right. A night in jail, without drugs and probably without sleep, had robbed Richard Blake of his will to resist. He was finished—used up. Defeat was plain in every blink of his eyes—in every nerveless, hopeless line of his body. At his forehead, the bandage was dirty and streaked with blood. He'd torn off the bandage that covered his hand, revealing an angry-looking gash, stitched in four places. His clothes were dirty and hung shapelessly on his thin body. His odor filled the small interrogation room. It was the familiar stench of sweat and dirt and body wastes, all mingled together in the unmistakable smell of fear and despair that permeates every corner of every police department in every country of the world. San Francisco's Hall of Justice was less than ten years old: a five-story glass-and-concrete cube. The interior was finished with brushed aluminum for the glitter, with white tile and plastic for the wear. When the building was new, some optimists had predicted that modern heating and air conditioning would beat the smell. But the pessimists had known better.

I pointed to the leather case, saying, "That's a lieutenant's badge, Blake. And I'm Lieutenant Hastings. I'm the one you tried to kill last night. Remember?"

"Aw, Jesus—" Shaking his head, Blake drew the back of his uninjured hand across his running nose. "Jesus, I told the other one—that Canelli. I was just trying to—"

"*Goddammit.*" I struck the table with the flat of my palm. This time he came half out of his chair. His lips began to quiver; his watery eyes first widened and then contracted, as if sudden pain racked his body. He began to tremble. His narrow body seemed to shrink, losing substance.

Secretly, I congratulated myself. Blake was ripe for the picking. I turned to the uniformed guard and gestured for him to leave. I'd already posted a homicide detective behind the two-way mirror, securing the observation room. If a visitor arrived—an assistant D. A. or a deputy chief—the inspector would use the red light to warn me. For what I intended to tell Richard Blake, I didn't want unfriendly witnesses.

Bracing my hands on the table, I leaned close to the suspect. His chair scraped the floor as he moved away from me. I dropped my voice to a low, dead-level note as I said, "It doesn't matter what you *thought* you were shooting at, Blake. All that matters is what I *say* you were shooting at." I let a beat pass as I looked down into his pale, twitching face. Then: "If I say you were trying to kill me, then that's how your indictment reads. Do you understand?"

He didn't respond, didn't look at me.

"That's why I wanted you to see the badge," I said softly. "I want you to know who you're dealing with. I want you to realize that it's my choice. If I say so, you're dead. It's up to me. Now—" I drew a deep, deliberate breath, at the same time straightening, stepping back, finally sitting in a small steel chair that faced the table. "Now, you've been through all this before. You know how it goes. You know I'm the one you talk to, if you want to help yourself. Do you understand?"

He sat huddled in his chair. He was hugging himself now, both hands clutching his scrawny biceps. He was staring fixedly at the table. Sweat covered his face.

Suddenly I reached forward, striking the table with all my strength. "*Answer* me, goddammit," I shouted.

Shuddering sharply, he desperately raised his watery brown eyes. "I—yes. I—I know what you mean. I understand." Timidly, he nodded. "But I—Jesus—I can't—" His voice trailed off as his eyes fell. Finally he whispered, "Listen, Lieutenant. I—Jesus—I'm a junkie. It—it's not a bad habit. Nothing heavy. But—" Hopelessly, he shook his head.

"I know you're a junkie, Blake. I know all about it." I let a long moment of silence pass while I watched him shivering, still hugging himself. Then, speaking softly, I said, "When you tell me what I want to know, I'll get you a methadone shot. I'll have you sent to San Francisco General. They'll take good care of you. They'll wash you up, and put you in a clean bed, and they'll give you a methadone shot. In an hour you'll be in heaven, Blake. All it takes is an order from me. Just my signature, on a piece of paper. That's all it takes."

Raising his head, he searched my face with desolate eyes, looking for some sign of hope. Finally, stammering, he said, "I already told him everything I knew. I swear to God, Lieutenant. I gave him everything I had."

"No, you didn't, Blake. You gave Canelli nothing. Crap. That's what you gave Canelli. Nothing but crap."

He began shaking his head in a loose, helpless arc. "No. I—I gave it all to him. You can check."

"I want the name of the one that hired you, Blake. And I want it now. Right now. Because if I don't get it—if I walk out that door without a name, then it's your ass. You'll fall for murder one. Never mind what you were shooting at last night. Forget that. Just think about that dead man in the back seat, with the ice-pick hole in his heart. Because he's all yours, Blake. If you won't help us— if we can't find the one who ran away—then he's all yours."

"But I—"

"You're stupid, Blake," I said quietly. "You don't even have intelligence enough to try and save yourself. You're about to fall for murder one. Nobody thinks you really committed the murder. You're too weak to do it. You're a small-timer—a nickel-and-dime hood. You don't have the intelligence to plan a murder. You don't have the guts, either. You're nothing. You know it, and we know it. But you're all we've got, Blake. So we'll take you. We'll put you away, no question. With your record you'll be inside until you're an old man." I paused, letting him think about it. Then: "It's your choice, Blake. You can fall for murder one—or you can fall for grand-theft auto. You choose."

As if he were trying to focus his gaze, he squinted and blinked, looking at me. He licked his lips before he ventured: "Grand-theft auto? Is that what you said?"

I shrugged. "If you cooperate—tell the whole story—you might not even get that."

"Not—not even that?" He spoke timidly, tentatively—as if he were a child, being offered candy from a stranger.

"It's like I said, Blake. You can have it the hard way or the easy way. Either you tell us the whole story—give us a name—or you don't. Your choice. But remember—" I pointed to the door. "If I walk out of here, you're dead."

"Either way, I'm dead," he muttered. "Either way."

"That may be. But that's your problem. I can help you with the law—maybe. But how you run the rest of your life, that's your problem."

Once more he began to shake his head helplessly. Suddenly it seemed as if I could see his whole desperate life revealed in his pale, formless face: the little kid without friends—the teen-age sneak thief—the contemptible bit of human flotsam that nobody wanted, everybody used. Like an insect, Richard Blake had been born to scuttle away from the light.

He knew it, too. The truth tore at his face like a spasm of mortal pain. I saw him close his eyes tight against the sudden anguish. With his eyes still closed, tears streaked his cheeks: two tears, one squeezed from the corner of each eye.

When his eyes came open, he was ready to talk. He sniffled and wiped at his nose with the back of his hand. Whenever I interrogated a junkie I carried Kleenex. Silently—waiting for him to talk—I handed over a tissue. He wiped his eyes, wiped his checks and then blew his nose. Dropping the tissue on the floor, he said, "His name is Thorson. That's all I know. Just Thorson. He—he gave me fifty bucks, like I said last night. He picked me up at the corner of Polk and Sutter, at quarter of ten. That was the whole thing—the whole deal. Everything. I swear it. I never saw him before he drove up. He told me what to do, and I did it. I did everything he said. The whole thing didn't take more than ten, fifteen minutes. He drove up, and asked me if my name was Blake. Then he slid over, and told me to drive. As soon as I got in, he gave me the fifty. He told me what to do—and I did it, just like I said. We went to the Beresford, and he told me to wait in the passenger zone." As he talked, his eyes darted uneasily around the room. Now, though, he looked directly at me. "Do you know where the Beresford is?" he asked anxiously.

I nodded. "On Sutter. Go ahead, Blake. Keep talking."

"Yeah. Well, he—he got out of the car. In front of the hotel. Thorson. And he went to a phone booth, about a half block away. He talked for maybe a minute, no more. Then he came back and got in the car. But this time he got in the back. He said that a guy was going to come out of the hotel, and he was going to get in the car. In back. When the guy got in, I was supposed to turn on the radio—music, real loud. I was supposed to turn the mirror up, too, so I couldn't see in back. Then I was supposed to drive down Sutter, and turn left on Kearny and then left on Columbus."

"And is that the way it happened? Just like that?"

He nodded fervently. "Just like that. The guy came out of the hotel and came right to the car."

"Did you see him—get a good look at him?"

He shook his head. "No. I wasn't supposed to look at him. I was supposed to look ahead. Straight ahead."

"Did you hear them say anything to each other?"

Again, he shook his head. "No. Nothing. I had the radio on, like I said. I didn't hear a thing."

"When did you first learn that Mur—that the passenger had been killed?"

"Not until the accident, Lieutenant. I swear to God."

For a long, silent moment I stared at him. Then, as if I wanted to believe him but couldn't, I slowly, regretfully, shook my head. "When there's a killing," I said, "there's noise."

"But there wasn't," he said plaintively. "I swear to God, there wasn't. Besides, I had the music on, real loud. It was rock music. I couldn't hear a thing."

Staring at him hard, I saw him struggle to meet my gaze, fighting desperately to convince me. Finally I decided to

42

say, "He was hit on the head. There was a fight, probably. You *had* to've heard something."

Letting his eyes fall, he gave up the struggle. Slowly, hopelessly, he shook his head.

So he was telling the truth. Only the truth, not believed, could defeat him so completely. He'd told me everything— almost.

"After the accident—" I said finally. "What happened then?"

Briefly he managed to meet my eyes, searching for hope. I didn't respond—didn't allow my face to change. I didn't want him to know that I believed him.

"As soon as we got hit," he said, "Thorson yelled at me to back up, and get out of there. But I couldn't. I couldn't go forward, because of the Mercedes. And a pickup hit us in our bumper, in back. He stayed there so I couldn't back up. The driver, he was hot. He started to get out of the truck. So then Thorson, he grabbed my shoulder, hard." As he spoke, Blake unconsciously touched his right shoulder. "He spoke real low, right in my ear. And his grip, I remember it was real strong. *Real* strong. And he said, 'There's a dead man back here—' Something like that. And all the time he's clamping onto my shoulder like you wouldn't believe. So then he tells me to run. 'Get out,' he says. 'Run. But don't attract attention.' Something like that. And then he opened his door, and he got out. So then I—Christ—I looked in the back, and saw the guy, dead. So then I— Christ—I ran. And you know the rest of it."

"How'd you happen to have a gun? You always bring a gun along with you?"

"Because I—you know—" He waved a slack hand. "I just carry a gun, most of the time. Because—" He hesitated, frowning. "Because what I do, it's dangerous. So I— carry a gun."

"What is it that you do, Blake?"

"Well, I—you know—I push a little of this and a little of that."

"Drugs, mostly?" I asked the question quietly, conversationally.

"Well—" Helplessly, he shrugged. "You know."

I nodded, letting a beat pass while he squirmed. Then: "Let's get back to Polk Street."

He looked at me warily. "Polk Street?"

"When Thorson picked you up. On Polk Street, you said."

"Oh. Yeah." He nodded. "Right."

"I want you to tell me exactly what he told you. Everything. Every word."

"Yeah. Well—" He frowned, earnestly puckering his eyes and furrowing his forehead. "Well, like I said, he told me the route—told me we were going to pick up someone at the Beresford. And —*oh yeah*—" He looked up at me, as if to ingratiate himself. "He said, 'The guy we're going to pick up owes me money. A lot of money. I'm going to have to talk to him.' Something like that." Now his expression was anxious as he scanned my face.

"Is that all?" I looked at him impassively.

"Yeah—" Disappointed, he dropped his eyes, and wiped his running nose. I handed him another Kleenex. "Yeah, that's all. Except for the streets, and the turns, that's all he said. That's every word."

In silence, I watched him wipe his forehead, wipe at his eyes and blow his nose—then drop the tissue on the floor. I let the silence continue until he began to move uncomfortably in his chair.

"You're sure that's all. You're positive. You've told me everything—the whole story. From beginning to end. Is that right?"

"Well—" He shrugged, spread his hands, shrugged again. "Well, yeah. Sure. That—that's right."

44

After another long, brutal moment of silence I sprang the trap: "How'd he know your name, Blake?"

"Wh-what?"

Elaborately patient, speaking slowly and distinctly, I said, "You just told me that before you got in the car, he knew your name. How?"

Unable to answer, he stared at me with round, foolish eyes.

"You're lying to me, Blake," I said softly. "You've been lying all along. You said you never saw him before he picked you up. But you also said he knew your name. How'd he know your name, if he'd never seen you before?"

"I—"

"Last night you told Canelli you *did* see him before. You told Canelli he stopped you on Mason Street. Right?"

"I—he—"

"Last night you were lying to Canelli. Either that, or you just lied to me. Isn't that right?"

"I—"

"*Isn't it?*" My hand crashed down on the table.

"I- -Jesus—yes. But—"

I rose from the chair and stood over him. I watched him struggling with it—trying desperately to think it through and save himself. Sweat glistened on his face. Unheeded, mucus streamed from his nose.

"Say hello to murder one, sucker." I turned and moved one slow, deliberate step toward the door—then another. Two more steps and I would reach the door. Playing out the bluff, I'd have no choice but to turn the knob and leave the room.

"No. Jesus. D—don't leave. Please, Lieutenant. *Please.* Jesus, don't leave."

At the door, I reached for the knob.

"He phoned me," he blurted. "Thorson phoned me, the night before. I swear to God. That's when he told me his name."

I stood with my back to him, contemplating the door-knob.

"He did. I swear it. He phoned."

I turned to face him. Folding my arms, I leaned against the door. Once more I saw truth tearing at his face.

"How'd he get your name?" I asked.

"He—I—I—don't know." But he couldn't meet my eyes as he said it.

"If I turn around, Blake, you've had it. If I go through that door, you're dead. I've told you once. I'm not going to tell you again."

Suddenly his body went slack. Sniffling—whimpering—he said, "I was in Kelley's, Tuesday night. That's a bar, on Mason. It—it's near O'Farrell."

"I know Kelley's."

"Well, there's—" He stopped speaking, gulped, then took the last hopeless plunge: "There's a bartender there. His name is Ricco. And he—he asked me if I wanted a job. And—" He shrugged. "And I said okay. I mean, I—you know—I haven't been doing so good, lately. So I—you know—" Helplessly, he broke off.

"You and Ricco had done business before. Is that it?"

His head bobbed loosely as he nodded. "Yeah. Right."

"What'd he tell you to do?"

"He—he just told me to go home and wait for a call. And I—I did. And that's all. I mean, I went home, and I waited. And about an hour later—about midnight, maybe—the phone rings. The guy says that his name is Thorson—that he's a friend of Ricco's. He asked me my name, and then he told me about the job, and what he'd pay, and everything. And I said okay. Then he told me where he'd pick me up, and when. And that was it. He just—just hung up."

"How'd he describe the job?"

"It was like I told you. He said a guy owed him money, and he was going to collect. And that's the whole thing. I swear, Lieutenant. That's all of it. Everything." As he spoke, his voice had dropped to a hoarse, exhausted whisper. Hunched over the table, sniffling, he was drained, beaten. He'd told it all. Silently, I gave him another tissue—then decided to leave the box.

"He'll off me, if he finds out," Blake muttered. "He'll kill me, for sure."

"Thorson?"

"No. Ricco."

Six

Just back from the Beresford Hotel, Canelli and Culligan were waiting for me in my office. In every respect, the two men were opposites. Culligan was a tall, thin, stoop-shouldered man with a long, morose face and mournful eyes. His nose was pinched, his cheeks hollow. His mouth was drawn down at the corners, permanently discouraged. His collars were always too large, his trousers too short. His face was sallow, sagging in sad, bassetlike folds. Culligan expected the worst from human nature and usually found it. He was resigned to evil.

"What'd you find out?" I asked the two men.

With his notebook already open on his bony knee, Culligan recited, "The subject, Eliot Murdock, checked into the Beresford Tuesday night at eleven-thirty. He gave his address as 3636 Occidental Boulevard, Los Angeles. He left a call for eight the next morning—yesterday, that is. At eight-thirty yesterday morning, he phoned New York—" Culligan held his notebook at arm's length, reading off the phone number. "That's the switchboard number for Barbour Publications," he said. "They publish *Tempo*. Manhattan South is checking to find out who he called. They'll get back to us." As he spoke, Culligan glanced at his watch, frowning. "They should've called by now. Anyhow, after he phoned, Murdock left the hotel. He took his room key with him. He didn't return to the Beresford until about eight that evening. There was at least one message in his box, the clerk remembers. At eight-thirty he made a call to—" Again, Culligan extended the notebook. "To 213-824-4076. That's a Los Angeles number for Barbara Murdock. Her address is 72818 Ralston Street."

"I tried twice to get her, just now," Canelli offered, "but she wasn't there. So then I called Los Angeles Homicide. And they said that they thought one of their guys was already looking for her. The way I understand it, they've already been to Murdock's place, and they got her name from Murdock's neighbor, or someone. Maybe it was the building superintendent. Anyhow, she's his daughter, I guess. But I figured that seeing as Los Angeles is already looking for her, I might as well let them. Unless you got other ideas, Lieutenant."

For a moment I stared at Canelli, marveling at his ability to make three words do the work of one. "Did you go over his room at the Beresford?" I asked, including them both in the question. "Really go over it?"

"Yes," Culligan answered firmly. "We didn't find anything, though. He was traveling light—just one suitcase and an attaché case. And those were already in the property room. All that was left in the hotel room was a newspaper, an airline schedule and an empty tube of toothpaste."

"Did you check what we have in the property room?"

"We just came from there," Canelli said. "There wasn't anything in the suitcase but clothes, so we left it in Property. Here's the attaché case—" He reached down beside his chair and lifted a black leather case to his lap. "There wasn't much in it, either, except for a checkbook and an airline itinerary from a travel agency. If the itinerary is right, then it looks like he flew from Los Angeles to Washington D.C. on Friday, and stayed in Washington until Tuesday. Anyhow, we're sure he flew American Airlines from Washington to San Francisco on Tuesday, because we already checked with American."

"When did he plan to leave San Francisco?"

"Tomorrow," Culligan answered.

"What's his checkbook look like?"

"If this is his whole financial story," Culligan said, flipping open the checkbook and riffling through the stubs, "it doesn't add up to much. The last deposit he made was six weeks ago, for thirteen hundred dollars. When he made the deposit he was down to a couple hundred." Culligan looked at the checkbook, reading: "He spent three twenty-five for rent—twice, in six weeks—a hundred three for insurance and three hundred for car repair. Now he's down to a couple hundred dollars again."

"Sounds about like my checkbook," Canelli said ruefully. "Pretty scratchy."

"He was well dressed, though," I said. "And he had a hundred eighty dollars on him, plus all the right credit cards. Also, Friedman says that a few years ago, Murdock was a well-known political columnist. He even had a TV program."

"Is that a fact?" As he said it, Canelli's swarthy, moon face brightened. "I'll be damned. A famous corpse, for a change."

"I never heard of him," Culligan observed sourly.

As they were speaking, I leafed through the lab's report on Murdock's room. Beyond "a probable eight different latent fingerprints," there was nothing in the report. Next I turned to the lab report on Walter Frazer's car. The preliminary survey showed six different sets of latent prints.

"What about Walter Frazer?" I asked. "Did you catch up with him?"

Canelli shook his head. "We went there first, just a little

after nine this morning. He lives in one of those big old town houses in Pacific Heights that's been converted into apartments. It's a pretty fancy place. He wasn't there, though. So we finally found one of his neighbors. She said she saw him get into a cab about a half hour before we got there. He's a lawyer, with an office downtown. We called down there. I guess it was about nine-thirty. But his secretary said he hadn't come in yet, and hadn't phoned, either."

"Was that unusual?"

Thoughtfully frowning, Canelli considered the question. "Well," he said finally, "she didn't *say* it was unusual. But that's the feeling I got. That it *was* unusual."

"What about Frazer himself? What'd the neighbors say about him?"

"We didn't do much about him," Culligan said. "We were mainly checking on his car. Why? Is he involved?"

I shrugged. "I don't know who's involved. Not yet. Except that I got a couple of names from Richard Blake."

Both men looked at me expectantly. While they took notes I outlined the information I'd gotten from Blake. As I talked I saw disappointment register on Canelli's face. He realized that Blake's testimony could provide information that might break the case. Since he'd conducted the basic interrogation of Blake, Canelli plainly wished that he'd been included in the second interrogation. Understandably, he felt upstaged by a superior.

". . . so what we've got to do," I finished, "is find Ricco, the bartender. Right now, he's the key. If he'll talk, we'll be closer to Thorson. So I want the two of you to go down to Kelley's and get to work on him. Before you leave, though, start someone on the phone, checking out Thorson. Let's start with the hotels and motels and airlines. I've got a feeling that he's from out of town."

"I know Ricco from when I was in Vice," Culligan said morosely. "He's heavy."

51

"Has he ever done any time?"

"I don't know whether he's done any time. But he's taken lots of falls."

"What for? What kind of falls?"

"Pimping, mostly. And receiving stolen goods, I think. He's got his finger in a little bit of everything."

"Then bring him downtown. Don't fool around with him out in the field. Bring him down, and we'll go to work on him. If you need help, get it. But I want him. He's seen Thorson, probably, face to face. I'd give odds on it."

"Maybe Blake was lying," Canelli said. As he spoke, his face brightened. Wishfully thinking, he transparently hoped that his initial interrogation of Blake would stand after all.

I shook my head. "I don't think so. He's scared of Ricco. Scared to death."

"I don't blame him," Culligan said wryly. "Ricco scares me, too. He's built like a tank." As he spoke, Culligan rose to his feet and went to the door, where he stood with his hand on the knob, waiting for Canelli. Standing stoop-shouldered in his ill-fitting clothes, eyeing Canelli with morose patience, Culligan looked like an undertaker waiting at the mortuary door.

"You want this, Lieutenant?" Canelli offered me the attaché case.

"No. Take it back to Property." As I spoke, my buzzer sounded. Waving goodbye to the two detectives, I flipped the intercom switch.

"There's a Walter Frazer in the reception room, sir. He's just come from Traffic Impound. He says he wants to talk to whoever's in charge of the Murdock homicide."

"Send him in." I gathered the reports and photographs into a single stack, then placed the manila folder on top. I was slipping into my jacket when an impatient knock sounded and Walter Frazer strode into my office. He was a man of medium height and medium-heavy build, about thirty-five years old. Behind sparkling gold-framed aviator glasses, his eyes were quick and shrewd. Advancing to shake my hand briskly, he walked with a firm and confident stride. Impeccably dressed in a conservative three-piece suit, Walter Frazer projected assurance, intelligence, vitality and fast-moving upward mobility. His hair was dark blond, thinning on top. He wore a thick guardsman-style mustache and sideburns to match. With its heavy jaw, broad nose and prominent brow ridges, his face gave the impression of strength and determination. A small double chin and a roll of flesh just above the collar suggested ten or fifteen pounds of extra weight. His handclasp was quick and hard—but his hand was pudgy, with a broad palm and stubby fingers. His fingernails were manicured.

"I'm sorry to bother you, Lieutenant," he said perfunctorily. "But the fact is that I can't get any answers, about my car. I can't even see it. So I decided to find the head man. You, I'm told."

I gestured him to a chair, and sat down behind my desk. "What can I do for you?"

He frowned at the question. "I should think that would be obvious." He chopped at the air with the edge of his hand, exasperated. "I want my car back. As soon as possible."

"Your car's at the crime lab, Mr. Frazer. It's evidence in a homicide, and it's impounded. I'm sorry, but you probably won't be able to get it back for another day, at least. The lab has to make sure their tests have been successful, before they can release it."

"What *tests* are you talking about?" Accenting the single word, his voice was heavily sarcastic.

"They're chemical and spectro-analysis tests, mostly." I spoke mildly, trying to calm him. "They're made on the contents of the car—dust samples, for instance, vacuumed from the floor. Sometimes, though, the lab shoots blanks. That's especially true of the spectrographic tests, where

53

they have to burn samples and analyze the results. By this afternoon, though, we should know where we stand. If there aren't any problems, the lab will probably release your car tomorrow. I'll release it, too. Then, after we get the D.A.'s release, you'll be all set. I'm sorry it's taking so long. But you're a lawyer, I understand. You know how important physical evidence is—and how tricky it is, too. Once we release that car, we can't take it back. The chain of evidence is broken."

For a moment he didn't answer, but simply sat staring at me. Plainly, he was struggling to suppress an angry reply. Every line of his body suggested frustration and impatience. Walter Frazer wasn't accustomed to being opposed.

"Will you notify me, personally, the moment the car is ready?" he asked truculently, at the same time snapping a business card down sharply on my desk.

I nodded. "I'd be glad to." I took the card, glanced at it, then slipped it into my desk drawer. "By the way—" I hesitated, waiting until he looked at me. "Were you told about the damage to your car?"

"It was a *slight* accident, I was told." His voice was sharp and suspicious. His eyes were narrowed. "A fender bender."

"That's correct."

"Did you see the car? Personally?" It was a brusque, contentious question.

"Yes, I did. The front fender is crushed. That's all."

"Is the car drivable?"

"The only problem might be that the fender is bent so it's touching the tire. However, if that's the case, I'd be glad to have the car taken to our garage. They can use a crowbar on it."

Eyes still shrewdly narrowed, mouth uncompromising beneath the bristling mustache, he considered the offer. Finally: "If there are any problems, I'll have a mechanic handle them. After all, the car's insured. Fully."

"Whatever you say, Mr. Frazer. Incidentally, while you're here, I'd like to get the details of how the car was actually stolen." As I spoke, I drew a note pad toward me and clicked a ball-point pen.

"I'm afraid," he said, consulting an expensive-looking watch, "that I don't really have the time. I've got a full calendar today. A very full calendar. And this thing hasn't helped, believe me." He looked at me accusingly, then added, "By the way, I've got to rent a car. Will the police department reimburse me for the time my own car is impounded?"

"I don't know," I answered carefully. "You should take that up with your insurance company."

"I will, believe me. You'll probably hear from them. Especially if your lab ties up the car for another day." Still staring at me with cold, accusing eyes, he gathered himself to rise from the chair. As he did, I raised a hand.

"Those details of the theft, Mr. Frazer—" I lowered my voice to a flat, official note. "I've got to have them, and as soon as possible. Unless you've got something that absolutely can't wait, I'd like to take your statement now. I realize that it's inconvenient—that this whole thing has been a lot of trouble for you. But I'd think, since you're here, that it would be simpler if you made your statement now. However—" I spread my hands. "However, if you'd rather, I can send one of my men along with you, to your office. Your choice."

Behind the sparkling gold-framed glasses, his eyes were baleful. Poised to rise, he'd gripped the arms of the chair, hard. Now, still gripping the chair, he forced himself to sit back. "I'm trying to explain to you, Lieutenant, that I'm a very busy man."

"So am I, Mr. Frazer."

For a moment we stared at each other, each silently testing the other's will. Finally he exhaled sharply and flung

55

another furious glance at the expensive watch. "All right. But make it fast."

"Thank you."

He didn't reply.

To needle him, I let a long, deliberate moment pass before I said, "First of all, exactly when was your car stolen?"

"Sometime between seven-thirty and ten-fifteen on Wednesday night," he answered promptly.

"Was the car in a garage?"

"Yes."

"Were the car keys in the ignition?"

He shifted impatiently. "As a matter of fact, they were." It was an exasperated admission. "I know better, but—" He let it go testily unfinished.

"We all make mistakes, Mr. Frazer."

He grunted. Plainly, he didn't think of himself as someone who made mistakes.

"I understand that you live in a town house that's been converted into apartments."

"That's correct."

"How many apartments are there in the building?"

"Three."

"And how many cars are kept in the garage?"

"Just one. Mine."

"Was the garage locked?"

"Yes. Certainly."

"Did you hear or see anything suspicious between seven-thirty and ten-fifteen?"

"Lieutenant Hastings"—he made a visible effort to suppress his impatience—"I've already been through all this, last night. You're obviously unaware of it, but two patrolmen came by about eleven-thirty. They—"

"I'm aware of it, Mr. Frazer. But they were investigating a car theft. I'm investigating a murder. And your car is evidence in that murder. Important evidence."

Fixing me with an angry look, he didn't reply.

To emphasize the point, I added, "According to our information, it's probable that whoever stole your car also committed the murder." I let a moment pass before I spoke again: "The murder was committed in your car, Mr. Frazer. In the back seat."

He still remained stubbornly silent. But, for the first time, I saw his gaze falter. He'd realized that his car—his property—had been tainted. Plainly, the idea displeased him. Walter Frazer was a fastidious man.

"Did you notice anything suspicious?" I asked quietly.

He shook his head. "No, nothing." It was a preoccupied response. His eyes drifted thoughtfully away. I saw him swallow. "Are there—" He cleared his throat. "Are there stains, on the back seat? Bloodstains?"

"I don't think so, Mr. Frazer. I'm not positive. But I don't think so."

"Well—" With a self-righteous hunch of his shoulders, he settled himself more firmly in his chair. "Well, I *hope* not."

It was a prissy, petty response, strangely at odds with his previous arrogance. For a moment I silently studied him, speculating on this unexpected change of character. Finally: "I gather that you put your car away at seven-thirty and discovered it was missing at ten-fifteen. Is that right?"

He nodded. "That's right." He spoke crisply. His assertive self-confidence had suddenly returned.

"How did you discover it was missing?"

"Well, I—" He gestured. "I went to get it, and it wasn't there. So I phoned you. The police, that is."

"You were going to go out, so you wanted the car. Is that what you mean?"

He drew a deep, impatient breath. "Naturally I was going to go out."

"Ten-fifteen seems late to be going out," I suggested.

"I was going out for cigarettes." Plainly exasperated, he spoke sharply, rudely. "It happens, you know."

"Was the garage door closed when you went to get the car?"

"Yes. Certainly."

"Why do you say 'certainly'?"

"Because it closes automatically. I have an electronic opener."

I nodded. Then, pretending puzzlement, I frowned. "Did you notice any marks of forced entry, Mr. Frazer? Was the garage door damaged, for instance? Was it sprung?"

"Not that I could see, no."

Still thoughtfully frowning, I said, "That would mean, then, that the thief must've had an electronic opener—identical to yours."

"Not necessarily," he answered promptly. "The patrolmen thought he came in through the service door. And I leave the opener in the car, naturally."

"You say that you'd left your keys in the car's ignition. Is that right?"

"That's right."

"Is there an inside door that leads from your garage to your apartment?"

"No."

"Then how did you get into your apartment?"

"How do you mean?" Suspicion sharpened his question.

"You said you left your keys in the car," I answered equably. "If your latch key was on the key ring, then you couldn't've gotten into your apartment." Staring at him, I let a beat pass before I said quietly, "Could you?"

For a moment he returned my stare. His eyes were impassive. I saw his hands tighten on the arms of his chair. Finally: "That was yesterday. Wednesday."

Nodding, I waited.

"My cleaning lady comes on Wednesday. She left the apartment door open, on the latch. Which is probably why I didn't realize I'd left my keys in the car. I didn't need them, to get into the house."

"Keys," he'd said, not "key."

But there'd only been one key in the Buick's ignition.

58

"Do you carry many keys on your key ring, Mr. Frazer?"

He shrugged. "The usual number, I suppose. Five or six." He glanced once more at his watch. "Listen, Lieutenant," he said, "I've really got to—"

"When we found your car," I said, "there was only one key in the ignition. We didn't find any other keys."

"You—" He looked at me with a sudden fixity. "You didn't?" As he said it, his right hand strayed toward his pocket—toward his keys, doubtlessly. I pointed to the pocket.

"Do you have your keys with you, Mr. Frazer?"

"They're my—my spare keys." He said it defensively, irritably. Then, repeating, "They're my spare keys. Naturally."

"Can I see them?" I asked pleasantly.

Momentarily he hesitated. Then he shifted sharply in his chair, withdrew a ring of keys from his trouser pocket and tossed the keys on the desk. I carefully examined the half-dozen keys.

"For spare keys," I said, "they look well worn." Slowly, deliberately, I placed the ring of keys on the desk before him.

Angrily, he snatched up the keys and rose quickly to his feet. Glowering down at me, he said, "Just what're you trying to say, Lieutenant?"

"I'm simply saying that—"

"You act like you're interrogating a—a murder suspect."

I got to my feet and we stood facing each other across my desk. "That's my business, Mr. Frazer," I said quietly. "Interrogating murder suspects."

"And my business," he fumed, "is conducting a law practice." For a long, furious moment, breathing hard, he glared at me, struggling to control himself. Finally: "I charge a hundred dollars an hour for my time, Lieutenant," he said, speaking in a low, tight voice. "Which means that this interview, so far, has cost me about seventy-five dollars." He thrust the keys in his pocket and turned to the door. "When you get my car ready for me, I expect you to call me. Or rather—" He jerked open the door. "Or rather, my secretary."

Seven

An hour later, just before noon, Canelli called from the field. "I just wanted to tell you, Lieutenant, that it looks like Ricco has split. Disappeared."

"Are you certain?"

"It sure looks like it, Lieutenant. He was supposed to show up at Kelley's at ten-thirty, to meet a couple of liquor salesmen. They were going to take him to a fancy breakfast, as I understand it. So then we went to his apartment. He lives with a woman named Gloria—who, if I have to say so, is really something else. I mean, me and Culligan decided we should do it by the book, just in case. So I took the fire escape, which by chance was off the bedroom, see. So there's this Gloria in bed, naked. And when she heard Culligan knock, she—"

"Canelli. Please. Forget the pornography, will you?"

"Oh. Sorry, Lieutenant. Well, anyhow, it turned out that Ricco called her last night about eleven, from Kelley's, and said something came up, and he might not make it home, but that she shouldn't worry, or anything. So right away she figured it was another woman, I guess. See, it turns out that Ricco and this Gloria have been living together for only about a month. So, naturally, she's jealous. Which is the reason we got her to talk so easy. Because she's jealous, I mean."

"When's Ricco due to go to work again at Kelley's?"

"Well, that's the goddamn trouble, Lieutenant. See, this is his day off. Thursday. He isn't supposed to come back on duty until five o'clock tomorrow night. Friday."

"Christ."

"Yeah."

"Thorson must've gotten to him. As soon as he left Vallejo and Columbus, Thorson must've phoned Ricco. And Ricco's hiding. The time fits."

"I know," Canelli answered heavily. "That's what Culligan and I figured, too. What a bummer."

"I want the two of you to stay on Ricco," I ordered. "Get two teams, on my authority, and have them stake out his apartment and the bar. Then you and Culligan go looking for him. He's probably holed up in the Tenderloin, somewhere. Culligan was in Vice. He knows his way around down there. Spread a little money around, if you have to do it. I'll cover you." As I spoke, my phone rang. "I've got to go, Canelli. Keep in touch."

"Okay, Lieutenant. Will do."

I lifted the phone and found myself talking to someone named Nevins, an assistant in the coroner's office. "What can I do for you, Nevins?" I asked.

"I understand that you're in charge of the Eliot Murdock homicide investigation."

"That's right."

"Well, sir, I thought I should tell you that his daughter, Barbara Murdock, is here."

"What's she doing there?"

"Someone down in Los Angeles told her to come here first, apparently, instead of to you."

I considered a moment, then asked, "Have you got someone who can bring her over here, to me?"

"Well—" There was a reluctant pause. Under a new,

cost-conscious municipal administration, each department poached on the other's manpower. It was taken for granted. Both Nevins and I knew that I should send a policeman for Barbara Murdock. But we both knew that Nevins was outranked.

"Yes, sir," he answered finally. "I guess we can do that."

"Good. Thanks, Nevins,"

"You're welcome, Lieutenant," he answered dryly.

I rose from my chair, circled my desk and gestured Barbara Murdock to a chair. She nodded when I introduced myself, and silently took a seat. I returned to my chair and sat for a moment without speaking, covertly studying her. She was about thirty years old, about a hundred fifteen pounds, about five feet two inches tall. Her hair was dark brown, cut short. Her face was oval, with a small nose, a firm mouth and a determined chin. Beneath dark brows, her brown eyes were calm and direct. The eyes were almond-shaped, almost Eurasian. The jaw was wide, the forehead broad beneath casually combed hair. Her neck was short and muscular. Altogether, it was an assertive, intelligent face—a face too strong to play the role of helpless female, and too independent to care.

"I'm sorry about your father, Miss Murdock. I understand he was well known—a TV personality."

For a moment she looked at me in thoughtful silence. Then, slowly and wearily, she smiled. "He would have liked to hear you say it. Not many people remember his TV shows. Especially on the West Coast." Her voice was low and even—an intellectual's voice, quiet and concise. As she spoke she crossed one leg over the other. She wore twill slacks and desert boots. Her thighs, I noticed, were firm beneath the twill. A brown suede leather jacket was belted at the waist, suggesting an exciting torso. At her throat, an orange silk scarf accented her brown eyes and olive complexion.

"Have you—" I hesitated. "Did you identify your father?"

"No. I—" She bit her lip. "I was told that someone had to—to be with me." With an effort, she kept her eyes raised, steadily meeting mine.

"Did anyone come with you? From Los Angeles, I mean?"

"No. There—" She hesitated. Then, still steadily meeting my gaze, she said, "There wasn't anyone to come." She spoke slowly, gravely—with a kind of desperate, lonely pride. Tears suddenly glistened in her eyes. But, instead of bowing her head, she managed to raise her chin.

"After we've—talked, I'll go the the coroner's with you," I offered. "They have rules over there. About people making identifications, I mean. They want someone with you."

"Thank you." She spoke softly, politely. And, finally, she lowered her gaze. She blinked, sniffled and futilely wiped at her eyes with long, graceful fingers. I opened a desk drawer, withdrew a box of Kleenex and silently pushed the box across the desk. For the first time she smiled at me. It was a tremulous smile—the smile of someone who badly needed a friend. For the first time I noticed a sprinkling of freckles across the upper part of her face. She blew her nose, wiped at her eyes and started to tuck the Kleenex tissue into the saddle-stitched leather handbag she wore slung over her shoulder.

"Before we go," I said, "I'd like to ask you some questions, if you don't mind." She blew her nose again, this time with an air of finality. "I don't mind," she answered.

Realizing that questioning a newly bereaved relative was always a race against memories and despair and tears, I took a moment to organize my thoughts before I said, "First, I'll tell you everything we know about your father's last—" I hesitated. "About his last few days."

Silently, she nodded. Now her eyes were clear. She shifted in her chair to face me fully, attentively.

"We think," I said, "that he went from Los Angeles to Washington Friday, and we assume that he stayed in Washington until Tuesday, when he came here to San Francisco. Is that right?" As I spoke, I pulled a note pad toward me.

"Yes."

"Did you know beforehand that he was going on this trip?"

"Yes."

"What was the purpose of the trip? Do you know?"

She hesitated, frowning as she considered the question. Finally: "It was a business trip." She spoke deliberately, guardedly. Her eyes had gone opaque. She was concealing something.

Because I didn't want to make it a contest so early in the interrogation, I shifted my ground: "When he left Los Angeles on Friday did you know his itinerary—cities, dates, hotels?"

"Yes. A travel agency worked out the itinerary for him. He gave me a copy."

Nodding, I pretended to make a notation while I considered her answers. Asked about her father's itinerary she responded readily, willingly. But when questioned about his business—about his reason for the trip—she grew cautious.

I let another moment of calculated silence pass before I looked up from the note pad and asked quietly, "Does the name 'Thorson' mean anything to you, Miss Murdock?"

"Thorson?" She frowned. "No. Nothing. Why?"

"Because," I answered, "we have reason to believe that he might have been involved in your father's death."

As I spoke I saw her eyes widen, as if she'd experienced sudden pain. Now she stared at me with a furious intensity. Gripping the arms of her chair, her hands were knuckle-white.

"You know who killed him?" she whispered.

I shook my head. "No, we don't. All we have is a suspicion. Not even that, really. All we've got is a name. It could be false. It probably *is* false."

"But at least you—" Painfully, she swallowed. The cords of her neck were drawn tight. "You have some idea. Something to work on."

"From all we've been able to determine, his death was planned. Carefully planned." I paused to let her think about it. She continued to stare at me with the same fixed, rigid intensity. Her mouth was tightly drawn, her nostrils pinched. Her breathing had quickened.

"Planned?" She seemed unable to comprehend it. Finally: "You mean it—it wasn't robbery? Or a—a mugging?"

"No, Miss Murdock. Your father was carrying about a hundred eighty dollars in cash. It wasn't taken."

"But—" She began to shake her head, as if the desperate, dogged movement could change what I'd said. "But I thought it was an—an accident. A—a random thing."

"It wasn't a random thing, Miss Murdock. Whatever else it was, it wasn't random."

"And this—this Thorson. He was the one who planned it?"

"That's what we think."

"But why?" Her voice was low, but the question boiled with repressed sibilance. Her eyes blazed. "*Why?*"

"We don't know why—we don't have a motive. That's the reason I'm asking you these questions. Because maybe you can help me find a motive. If we know why he died, we're a lot closer to discovering who killed him."

I watched the blaze in her eyes fade. The corded muscles of her neck smoothed; her hands relaxed their death-grip on the chair. "It must've been the story," she said. "That must've been it. I never—it never occurred to me. But—" She broke off, and began slowly, hopelessly shaking her head.

66

I knew I had only to wait for her to tell me what I needed to know. I sat quietly, watching her struggle with the knowledge that her father's murder wasn't an accident—that her father could have caused his own death.

"It was going to be his comeback," she said softly. She paused, drawing a deep, unsteady breath. As if her body had suddenly lost its strength, her hands dropped from the chair to her lap. Haltingly, her fingers sought each other, finally clasping loosely together. Her eyes fell, studying the helpless hands. "That's what he called it—his comeback." She drew another shaky breath, then continued in a dull, defeated monotone: "Fifteen or twenty years ago, when I was still a little girl, Dad was very—very successful. He was never a major columnist—not like Reston, or Walter Lippmann. But he had a following. He was good at what he did. Very good. But then—" As if she were lifting something very heavy, she slowly raised her shoulders. "Then maybe he started to believe his own publicity. He was very good at that, too—at getting publicity for himself. Anyhow, for whatever reason, Dad and Mom started to fight. Later, after they couldn't hurt each other any more, they started to have love affairs. In Washington it was very easy to have affairs, especially for a man like Dad. So then, inevitably, came the divorce. That was eleven years ago. Dad was forty-six, and Mom was forty-two. I was still in college, when they both drove up and told me. And then—" She broke off. Still bowed over her hands, she began to shake her head.

"And then, a few months later, Mom killed herself in an auto accident. So after that, Dad started to drink. He— he'd always drunk a lot. Every night before dinner—when he was home—he'd drink four or five martinis. Sometimes more. And it never bothered him—never got the best of him. But after Mom's accident it started to bother him. It got the best of him. One drink, and he was drunk. Overnight, it seemed, his whole life came apart. He didn't keep appointments, and he let someone else write his columns. On TV, he couldn't even follow the Teleprompter. So—" She lifted one hand in a wan gesture of resignation and defeat, then let the hand fall back in her lap. "So, inside of two years, he was out. Nobody renewed his contracts. And he didn't seem to care. All he cared about was drinking, it seemed. I—I tried everything. I was out of college by then, and for a while we lived together. But I couldn't stand to see him ruining himself, and I told him so. I told him that I was going to take the money I'd inherited from Mom, and I was going to get as far away from him as I could. And that's what I did. I went to Los Angeles, where I had friends, and I've been there ever since. I told him when I left Washington that he was welcome to come to Los Angeles. He was welcome to stay with me. But not if he drank. Never if he drank."

"And is that what happened? He went to Los Angeles? And quit drinking?"

Slowly, somberly, she nodded. "Yes," she answered gravely, "that's what happened. He finally quit drinking. And—finally—he started writing newscasts, for third-rate radio stations. After a year, though, he had his own program. Another year, and he was back on TV, on a local Los Angeles station. But—" She sighed regretfully. "But he'd always had Potomac fever. He'd had power once, and he wanted it again. That's what Potomac fever is—an obsession with power. It's an addiction. You never get over it." She paused. I saw the shadow of an exhausted smile cross her face—then twist into a bitter spasm. "I guess it killed him finally."

I decided not to respond. I knew that soon her strength would fail. The reality of death was beginning to numb her. I didn't want her to waste even one word, responding to a meaningless expression of condolence from me.

When she began speaking again, her voice was hardly more than a hoarse whisper: "About three months ago," she said, "he got a tip from someone in Washington. I don't know the details. He's always been—" She broke off, blinked, drew a sharp, hard breath. Momentarily her eyes blanked as she forced herself for the first time to make the stark, terrible correction: "He *was* always very secretive about his stories—especially the big stories. But, at the same time, he'd test my reactions, sometimes. So I pieced some of it together."

"That's the story he was working on, in Washington?"

She nodded. "I'm almost sure of it."

"What did the story involve?"

Wryly, she smiled. "The usual. Influence peddling. Cover-ups. Graft in high places. In Washington, no cocktail party is complete without the rumors. Usually they all evaporate. But this time, apparently, Dad was on to something big. As I say, he couldn't resist telling me some of it. He had someone important in his pocket. He told me that much. He had someone who knew where the bodies were buried, and who was willing to talk about it."

"Was one of the bodies buried in San Francisco?"

"I don't know," she answered. "I really don't have any idea. But I'm almost sure that he came here to run down part of the story."

"Where'd he stay, in Washington?"

"At the Hilton."

"How many times had he gone to Washington, working on the story?"

"Twice. Once a month ago, and once about three months ago."

"Did he always stay at the Hilton?"

"Yes. If you're in the media business, free-lancing, you've got to stay in the right hotels. You've got to eat in the right restaurants, too. Especially in Washington."

"Do you work in the media, too, Miss Murdock?"

Wearily, she shrugged. "It depends on what you mean

by the media. I'm a script supervisor at MGM. I free-lance, too. And I've also written a couple of TV scripts."

I smiled at her. "I'm impressed."

She tried to return the smile—but failed. As if the effort had cost her too much, she slumped back in the chair, momentarily closing her eyes. She'd suddenly come to the end of her strength. I rose, locked my desk and quietly suggested that we go to the morgue.

Eight

"Did you see this?" Friedman tossed a copy of the *Sentinel* on my desk before he sank into my visitors' chair. "It's on the front page, in a box at the bottom."

"*Commentator Slain in North Beach Murder*," the headline read. Quickly, I skimmed the story, continued on the back page of the main news section. Revealing neither too much nor too little, the details of the murder were almost exactly as I'd given them to the *Sentinel's* police reporter earlier in the day. Making a mental note to thank the reporter, I continued to read. Eliot Murdock, I learned, had started his career in Los Angeles, beginning as a general-assignment reporter. During World War II he'd been a war correspondent in Europe and had been wounded in Normandy. After the war he'd gone to Washington, working as press secretary for a California congressman. Later he'd moved up to administrative assistant. When the congressman was defeated at the polls, Murdock parlayed his congressional connections into a "long-running inside-Washington column." The article dealt briefly with Murdock's career and finished with a reference to his daughter, a "fast-rising Hollywood screen writer." Nothing was said about Murdock's comeback try, or about his possible reasons for being in San Francisco.

"I'll give even money," Friedman said, "that this is only the first of many, many articles on Eliot Murdock."

"Why do you say that?"

"Two reasons—" He raised a thick forefinger. "First, there's nothing the press does better than eulogize one of its own, especially if the dead Indian died more or less in the line of duty. It's one of those unwritten laws. And, second—"Another finger joined the first. "Second, if there's anything to this Washington scandal story—anything at all—it's going to sell many, many newspapers. Believe it."

"I believe it."

"So you'd better start wearing clean shirts to the office," Friedman said. "Because you might make the Walter Cronkite show. Who knows?"

I didn't reply. But secretly, I hoped he was right.

"And then we've also got the hired hit-man angle," Friedman said. "That's always good copy."

"What hired hit man?"

"Thorson," he answered casually. "I'll bet you a five-dollar lunch, right now, that Thorson—or whatever his name is—was imported for this job. I'll bet he was paid a fat fee and flown in from somewhere else. Is it a bet?"

"Where're you getting all these theories? I thought you were on that Hunter's Point thing."

"I am. But Hunter's Point is just your normal, grisly, big-city-type drunken, psychotic, week-in-and-week-out, spur-of-the-moment homicide. Murdock is a different matter altogether. Is it a bet?"

"What makes you so sure Thorson's a professional?"

"That compress, mostly," he answered promptly. "The ice pick, we all know about. It's neat—no muss, no fuss. Which is why the Mafia, to drop a name, favors ice picks. But that compress—" Friedman nodded emphatic ap-

72

proval. "That's fastidious. And besides being fastidious, it also shows planning—right down to the last drop of blood."

"Maybe there's more than fastidiousness involved."

"How do you mean?"

"Let's suppose that it was a carefully planned hit, which seems likely. And let's assume that Thorson picked up the car, which he apparently did, and hired a wheelman, which he apparently did, and proceeded to kill Murdock for a fat fee—which he probably did. Now, if that's the way it went, then why was he so careful about the blood?"

Friedman's thick eyebrows drew together in an elaborate frown. I knew why he was frowning. Friedman liked to ask the questions, not answer them. Finally, grudgingly, he said, "I give up. Why?"

"Maybe the car wasn't really stolen," I said, not without a small, secret sense of smug satisfaction. "Maybe he intended to return the car."

Approvingly, Friedman nodded. "That I like," he announced. "That's a twist with class. Are you going to pursue it?"

"I'll have Canelli and Culligan check Walter Frazer out. I was going to do it anyhow. Some of his reactions didn't quite add up."

"Good. Keep me posted. Well—" Ponderously, he heaved his two hundred thirty pounds out of the chair. "Back to the Hunter's Point Murder Case. In a couple of hours, though, I should have it all tied up and dropped on the D.A.'s desk. So I'll be able to lend a hand."

"Good."

When he'd gone, I leaned back in my chair and closed my eyes. The time was almost four o'clock. So far, it had been a fruitless, frustrating day. I'd spent almost two full hours with Barbara Murdock, time I could ill afford to lose. After she'd identified her father's body, Barbara had decided to stay in San Francisco until she could take possession of the body. When she learned that her father had stayed at the Beresford, she wanted to stay in the same hotel. I had no choice but to drive her to the Beresford and get her settled.

During our two hours together I began to realize that Barbara Murdock was a remarkable woman. She was intelligent and determined—and tough, too, with a quiet, stubborn courage. At the morgue they'd shown us into a small, sterile viewing room. I began explaining the identification procedure, but Barbara already knew. She'd once worked on a documentary called *Death in the City*, she'd said. She walked directly to the large, heavily curtained window— and waited. Almost angrily, she shook off the touch of my hand on her arm. "He was all I had," she'd whispered fiercely. "There wasn't anyone else. Leave me alone."

After she'd made the identification she turned her back on me and surrendered to a spasm of dry, wracking sobs. She stood with shoulders hunched in pain, arms clasped across her stomach, leaning her forehead against the pale green wall. Between sobs she gasped out a vow of vengeance. She would discover who had killed him, she said, and she would see them dead. When I promised to help her, she hardly seemed to hear me.

Finally she'd pushed herself away from the wall, turned, and asked me for a handkerchief. Driving to the Beresford, composed, she asked me how we intended to find her father's killer. I'd tried to be honest with her—tried to explain that it takes time and work and luck to catch a murderer—and patience, too. Both of us, I said, must be patient.

It had been a mistake. After she signed the Beresford's guest register, she turned to me. "I don't want to be patient, Lieutenant," she said softly. "I want to find out who killed my father. And I *will* find out. Believe me, I'll find out." Then she'd politely thanked me for everything I'd done, turned away and walked to the elevators. Her stride had been firm, her back straight, her head high.

74

She would do it, I realized wearily. She would try to find out who murdered her father.

I was about to dial Communications, trying to get through to Canelli, when the receptionist called to announce Mr. Jeffrey Sheppard, "inquiring about the Murdock homicide." From the tone of the receptionist's voice, it seemed that Jeffrey Sheppard was someone important— and someone in a hurry.

I was right. Jeffrey Sheppard snapped down an embossed business card on my desk and took a seat without being asked. He was a big, impressive-looking man with broad shoulders, a thick neck and the broadly sculpted head of a Roman centurion. His age was about forty-five. He was expensively dressed in a tweed jacket, cavalry twill trousers and a soft wool turtleneck shirt. As he sat hunched truculently in his chair, he reminded me of a big, tough, bull-shouldered linebacker sitting on the bench, straining to get back into the mayhem of a football game.

Glancing down at the card, I read: Jeffrey Sheppard, Managing Editor, *Tempo* magazine. It was a Park Avenue address.

"What can I do for you, Mr. Sheppard?"

"I have—had—Eliot Murdock under contract," he answered, speaking in a deep, rich, melodious voice. As he spoke, the linebacker image faded—replaced by that of the board chairman, dominating a directors' meeting.

"*Tempo* has exclusive rights to the material Murdock developed," he said. "I'm having copies of the contracts flown out from New York to verify the point. I've also retained a local lawyer."

"I'm not sure I know what you're getting at, Mr. Sheppard. What's the lawyer for?"

Impatiently, he sighed: a sudden sharp, contemptuous exhalation. The message was clear. Jeffrey Sheppard didn't have time for inferiors who asked obtuse questions. "For the past three months," he said, "Murdock has been working on a story of high-level graft at the Pentagon." He paused, eyed me for a moment, then added, "That's in Washington."

"I know where it is."

As if he hadn't heard me, he continued speaking in the same deep, resonant voice: "Our contract with him entitles us to all the material he's developed during his inquiries. We paid an initial fee on signing the contract, with the balance due upon receipt of a satisfactory manuscript. That, obviously, we will never get—at least, not from Murdock. However, Murdock must have taken notes on everything he discovered—every interview, every bit of research. He probably had those notes with him when he arrived here in San Francisco. Under the terms of the contract, those notes are ours. That's why I'm here."

I looked down at his card. "Did you come from New York?"

"No. Of course not," he answered sharply. "I was in Los Angeles when I heard the news of Murdock's death. I flew up. Just now."

"Have you been in touch with Murdock's daughter?"

"His daughter?" Sheppard's eyes narrowed. "Is she here?"

"Yes."

"Does she have the notes?"

"As far as I know, Mr. Sheppard, there aren't any notes. There weren't any notes on Murdock's body or in the car where he was murdered. And there weren't any notes in his luggage, either."

"Was his murderer captured? Could he have them?"

"Before I answer that, I'd like to ask you a few questions, Mr. Sheppard. If you don't mind."

"Of course I don't mind." But the edge to his voice and the impatient shift of his shoulders contradicted his words.

"First, how'd you learn of Murdock's death?"

"It was on the AP wire, this morning. It came into our

office in Los Angeles. Of course, I was informed immediately." He flicked back his sleeve and looked at his watch.

"The next question is, how much can you tell me about the story Murdock was working on?"

As I asked the question I saw his expression change. He eyed me for a brief, shrewd moment before he said, "At the moment, Lieutenant, I'm not prepared to respond to that point. I want to see the notes first."

Again, the message was clear. If he didn't get the notes, I wouldn't get the information I needed.

"We may never find those notes, Mr. Sheppard. In the meantime, I've got a murderer to catch. And it's possible that Murdock's death was connected to the story he was doing for you. So I need all the information I can get about the investigation Murdock was conducting. The sooner the better."

For a moment he eyed me with calm, cold calculation. Then: "We've got different stakes in this, Lieutenant. You're trying to catch a murderer. I'm trying to put together what could be the biggest news story of the year. I've got to protect that story. I can't afford any leaks."

I felt myself becoming angry. "You're telling me that you refuse to give me the information. Is that right?"

"I'm telling you that it's my responsibility to protect my news sources—and to protect the independence of the press." He spoke calmly and superciliously, as if he were explaining a simple problem to a slow learner.

"And *I'm* telling *you* that I want that information."

He didn't bother to reply; his silence was eloquent. For another long, hostile moment we stared at each other. Finally, speaking slowly and distinctly, I said, "From all you've said, Mr. Sheppard, I gather that you're a very busy man. Your time is valuable. Is that right?"

Deliberately—insolently—he nodded. "That's right, Lieutenant." He watched me intently—as a fighter watches his opponent between flurries.

"Well, then," I said, "you should realize that you could have a problem."

"A problem?" It was an amused response. His broad, expressive mouth twitched in a patronizing smile. So far, he'd found me an inferior antagonist.

"Right. A problem. You admit you have information that's vital to my investigation. That makes you a material witness. If you refuse to divulge that information, I can place you in custody for the purpose of protecting that information."

The patronizing smile took a slow, ugly twist. "I think that would be a very brave thing for you to do, Lieutenant. Brave, but foolhardy. Because you'd be starting something you couldn't finish."

Realizing that I couldn't afford to lose my temper, I drew a long, deep breath. "You may be right, Mr. Sheppard. I've got a better idea." I pointed to the phone. "If you continue to refuse cooperation, I'm going to call the D.A.'s office and recommend that you be charged with withholding information in a murder investigation. Obstructing justice, in other words. If the D.A. goes along with me—and I think he will—you'll be indicted and brought to trial."

"That's bullshit and you know it." His voice was silkily malicious; his eyes gleamed with the pleasure of combat— and the anticipation of certain victory.

"We'll see." I locked my eyes with his—and waited. It was all I could do: wait, and hope he didn't challenge me to pick up the phone.

"If I had the time," he said, "I'd enjoy seeing the D.A.'s reaction to this little charade of yours. I'd like to see him slap your wrist. Publicly."

I didn't reply. Having committed myself to silence, I had no choice—no more options. And finally, I thought I saw a shadow of hesitation flicker deep in his eyes. "If I had the time," he'd said. Possible meaning: he might be giving himself a face-saving way out.

"I'd like to try you, Lieutenant," he said softly. "If I didn't have to be in New York tomorrow night, I'd like to try you. I really would."

I decided not to respond—not to goad him. If he needed a way out, I would oblige him. If he chose to taunt me with his boardroom sneer, I was willing to take it.

I saw him glance one last time at his watch. It was the final move in the silent, savage little game we were playing. All that remained was a small, contemptuous curling of his lip, signifying that I was an opponent unworthy of his best blows. When I offered no dissent, he began speaking with offhand scorn: "The fact is—the *truth* is—that I really don't know much about Murdock's story. Which is precisely why I want his notes. All I know is that he came to see me a little more than three months ago, in New York. He said that he'd been in contact with a middle-level Pentagon official. I gathered that the official was about to be either fired or demoted. In any case, the official was bitter. Very bitter. He'd known Eliot for years—since boyhood, I gather. So he contacted Eliot and said he had information on a kickback scheme that could go all the way to the top."

"What'd he mean by 'the top'?"

"He meant the top of government—the Pentagon, the Senate, possibly even the White House."

"But he didn't name names."

"I assume," Sheppard said, "that he named names to Eliot. But Eliot didn't pass on the names to me."

"Why not?"

"He didn't want to take a chance on leaks."

"Did he tell you how the kickback scheme would operate?"

"Just in general terms. It had something to do with surplus military hardware. That's all Eliot would tell me."

"When was the last time you talked to Murdock, Mr. Sheppard?"

"He called Monday, from Washington. He said that he

got everything he needed in Washington. Which makes me think that he might've gotten affidavits."

"What else did he say when he called Monday?"

"He said that he was leaving the next day for here—for San Francisco."

"Why San Francisco?"

"I don't know," Sheppard said, speaking with a note of unmistakable finality. "Except that he said San Francisco might be the last stop."

"The last stop?"

"That's right, Lieutenant," Sheppard said, rising from the chair and buttoning his elegant jacket. "That's what he said—the last stop. As it turned out, he was right." With an imperious gesture, Sheppard pointed to his card, still lying on my desk. "Hold on to that," he ordered. "I expect to hear from you. I'll be at the Mark Hopkins until tomorrow afternoon. Then I'll be at my office in New York." He turned abruptly and left the office. I didn't get to my feet to see him out.

Nine

Waiting for news from the FBI's fingerprint division in Washington, I stayed at my desk until nine that night. For hours I'd been trying to assemble all the tangled skeins of the Murdock case into some kind of coherent pattern. I hadn't had much success. With most of the lab reports complete, the results were predictable—and disappointing. After eliminating fingerprints known to be Murdock's and Blake's, the lab indentified at least four other sets of latent prints found in the murder car. One set probably belonged to the murderer. The other two sets probably identified garage mechanics, friends of Frazer's or complete strangers. An hour ago, CBI at Sacramento had called to say they didn't have prints on file that matched the prints on the compress wrappings. Now Washington was our last hope.

At about eight, Canelli and Culligan returned from the field—empty-handed. Ricco had apparently vanished without a trace. With more than half the hotels checked, the three detectives working the phones hadn't found any trace of Thorson. Making it a request, not an order, I asked Canelli and Culligan to check out Walter Frazer's movements last night. They agreed to canvass Frazer's neighbors for an hour or two before they went home to bed. Then, tomorrow, they could begin checking out Frazer's business activities.

After eating vending-machine sandwiches and coffee with Friedman, I put a call through to Richard Blake, at the County Hospital. He'd gotten his methadone shot and greeted me like an old friend. But when he learned that Ricco had disappeared, he became agitated. "Are you going to let me go?" he asked.

"Isn't that what you want?"

"Not with Ricco loose, that's not what I want," he answered. "No way."

"I've got to charge you or release you in forty-eight hours."

"Forty-eight hours?"

"Forty-eight hours."

"Jesus."

At that moment my other line blinked. Pressing the illuminated button, I heard an elegantly English-accented woman's voice coolly announce that Avery Rich, the publisher and sole owner of the *San Francisco Sentinel*, wanted to speak with me. I'd once been told that west of the Mississippi, only a handful of men were more powerful than Avery Rich.

His voice was thin and dry: an old, brittle instrument, but one still finely tuned—still a marvel of impersonal precision. "I've just talked with Jeffrey Sheppard, Lieutenant Hastings." He waited for me to answer.

"Yes, sir."

"I know of your reputation, Lieutenant. I believe you to be a conscientious policeman—and a man of intelligence and integrity."

"Thank you."

"Which is why I'm calling you before I call the mayor. I want to tell you what I intend to tell him." There was a brief pause. In the background I thought I heard chamber music. "I'm going to tell the mayor," the precise voice continued, "that I'd like to see our police department extend Mr. Sheppard every courtesy and consideration. I'm telling you this for two reasons, Lieutenant. The first reason is that I've never believed in going over a man's head without telling him first. And the second reason is that I want to make it very clear, both to you and to the mayor, that I expect the same consideration for Mr. Sheppard as I expect for myself. Do you understand?"

"Yes, sir, I do."

"Good. You're working late. Are you working on the Eliot Murdock case?"

"Yes, sir, I am."

"Are you making progress?"

I considered, then said, "At this point in the investigation, I'd say we're making normal progress."

It was Avery Rich's turn to pause before he said, "That sounds like an honest answer, Lieutenant. It sounds neither fatuous nor self-serving nor craven. It sounds about right."

"Thank you."

"Eliot Murdock was a second-rate journalist. I met him once and didn't like him. He lacked depth, and it showed in his work. He lacked grace, and he lacked command of the language. He was too anxious for success—in too much of a hurry. And that showed, too. Quite plainly."

I decided not to reply.

"Still, he was an honest man. And, with all his shortcomings, Eliot Murdock had a by-line. He had his own audience. His voice was heard—and recognized. Which is to say that, in death, his faults will be forgotten and his virtues enlarged, especially if it serves the purposes of others. Do you understand what I'm saying?"

"I think so, sir."

"Good. I hope, when you've solved the case, you'll come

by my office. I'd like to meet you—and thank you personally. Call my secretary. She'll remember you."

"Thank you."

"You're welcome, Lieutenant. How old are you?"

"Forty-four."

I thought I heard him sigh. "My daughter is forty-three.
She's just called to say she's divorcing her third husband.
Good night, Lieutenant." The line went dead.

I hung up the phone, looked at it for a moment, then
lifted the receiver again and asked the operator to get me
Barbara Murdock, at the Beresford Hotel.

Across the small Formica table, Barbara Murdock
drank the last of her scotch and water and gravely placed
the empty glass on the table before her. It was her second
drink in less than twenty minutes.

"I shouldn't do that," she said. "Not tonight."

I didn't reply.

"You don't drink." She gestured to my half-empty glass
of tonic water.

"No."

"Did you ever drink?"

"Yes," I answered slowly. "I used to drink. A lot. Too
much, in fact."

For a moment she looked me full in the face, frankly
appraising me. Finally she said, "You have the look of a
man who—" Still assessing me, she broke off, thinking.
Then: "You look like a man with something on his mind.
Something that's been on his mind for a long time."

I smiled. "Doesn't everyone?"

"No," she answered, "everyone doesn't. Everyone
should. But everyone doesn't. Most people forget things
they shouldn't forget. That's the great gift the media con-
fers on us. It lets us forget. Which explains why Americans
are people who don't have past tenses to their lives. All
we've got is the future. And it scares us. It scares us silly."

"You're a very philosophical lady."

"And I suspect that you're a very philosophical man."

"Thank you. Do you want another drink?"

"Yes," she answered. "So I'm not going to have one. But thanks."

"You're welcome."

"Why are we here, Lieutenant? You haven't told me. Not really."

As concisely as I could, I outlined Jeffrey Sheppard's visit. As I talked, her eyes never left mine. When I finished, she said, "I remember meeting Jeffrey Sheppard. I was only a little girl, not more than ten years old. But I remember thinking that he was a real prick."

I laughed out loud. "Do little girls use words like that?"

"Only when someone like Jeffrey Sheppard comes along."

"Still, he gave me something to think about. It sounds like your father's notes are missing. Maybe some affidavits, too."

Staring off across the small cocktail lounge, she smiled: a sad, wistful twisting of her small, determined mouth. "Dad would love all this. He was very good at building the suspense—at keeping people guessing." She let a pensive moment pass, then added, "I suppose, really, that he was a little paranoid. Most secretive people are." For a moment she sat silently, idly turning her highball glass in its own wet circle on the Formica tabletop. I found myself looking at her long, tapering fingers, curved so gracefully around the glass. Barbara Murdock was a small woman, compactly made. To match her body, the hands should have been small, with short, stubby fingers. If the body expressed the personality, then perhaps the difference between her hands and her stature reflected the contradictions in her nature. Because, certainly, she was a study of opposites.

"He was really a pretty pathetic person," she said softly. "He was driven by vanity and insecurity and power lust, all rolled into one big, messy ball. He was really a small, frightened person—like the rest of us. Even when he was on top of the heap—or, at least, his particular heap—he was always looking over his shoulder." Again, she paused before she said softly, "I always secretly despised him for looking over his shoulder. But now I realize that most ambitious people look over their shoulders. It goes with the territory."

"Do you look over your shoulder?"

For a long, speculative moment she looked at me before she said, "Yes. Don't you?"

"I suppose so. In my business there's always someone who can run faster and hit harder and shoot straighter. That's what my business comes down to—running faster than the bad guys."

"What did you do, before you were a policeman?"

"Mostly I was a football player—a professional football player for the Detroit Lions. Then, after a couple of knee operations, I took a job in my father-in-law's factory. Which turned out to be a mistake."

"Are you married?"

"I was."

"I was, too," she said quietly. "I've been divorced for longer than I was married. Until today, somehow, I never thought much about it. The last few hours, though, I can't seem to think of anything else." She shrugged. "Maybe it's just as well."

"How long were you married?"

"Three years." She sat silently for a moment, staring down at the table between us. "Until tonight I never really regretted it. Getting divorced, I mean. But now—" She broke off and shook her head, softly sighing. Then: "Tonight, I'm dreading that empty bed."

"I know that feeling, too."

"She raised her gaze and looked at me with frank appraisal. "Do you?" It was an invitation: an eye-to-eye suggestion that we might help each other through a lonely night—one lonely night.

As I looked into her eyes I remembered my own lonely nights. After my divorce—after my escape from Detroit—I'd tried all the combinations: the bars, the bottle, the long nights alone with the TV. There'd always been women—but never the right woman. I'd always known that the fault was mine, not theirs. I'd always realized that since my divorce, I couldn't get a handle on myself—couldn't begin to understand who I was, or what had happened to me. Separated by only a year, the end of my playing career had coincided with the end of my marriage. At first, it had been easy to blame my wife. Carolyn had been a blond, beautiful, predatory socialite. For purposes of her own, a football player had been exactly right: a cunningly contrived contrast to the rest of her life. Later, complementing what seemed to be a picture-perfect marriage, we'd had children. The boy, Darrell, looked like me: heavily built, with big hands, regular features and serious eyes. Almost fifteen years old, Darrell was struggling with an identity crisis, keeping his problems to himself. Claudia resembled her mother: a willful, intelligent, wonderfully proportioned girl. Claudia was almost seventeen—and hated her stepfather. Someday, she said, she'd move to San Francisco. Whenever I heard her voice on the long-distance phone, I wondered whether the time had come.

I realized that I was still staring at Barbara—and she was staring at me. I decided to look away—to murmur something trivial—to decline her unspoken invitation.

Because, less than a year ago, I'd met Ann—and my life had changed. I didn't know how it had changed. I realized that I might never know. But I knew Ann was the reason.

Across the table Barbara Murdock was smiling: a small, lonely, infinitely regretful smile. But it was a friendly smile, too. The smile confirmed that, subtly and silently, we'd become friends. Never lovers. But friends.

"You're a—" She hesitated. Then: "You're an understanding man."

"Thank you."

"What time is it?"

I glanced at my watch. "A little after ten."

"Do you have men still—" She bit her lip. "Still working on my father's murder? Besides you?"

"Yes. Several men."

She nodded. "Good. Thank you."

"You're welcome. But I have to be honest. We aren't doing it for you. Or, at least, not entirely for you."

"I know. You're doing it as much for the Jeffrey Sheppards of the world as you are for me."

Regretfully, I answered her nod. "In a way you're right. It's sad but true."

"I've been thinking about Dad's notes," she said. "And I remembered something." I waited for her to go on. "He always carried one of those salmon-colored expanding envelopes," she said thoughtfully. "The kind that's used for legal papers, and has a string. It was a—a thing with him. One of his trademarks. He always carried it in his inside jacket pocket. He always hated to carry a briefcase."

"If he was carrying it on him," I said, "then the murderer took it."

"I doubt if he'd carry it on him—not at night. Not in a strange city. Dad was always very careful. He got mugged once, in Washington. After that, he was supercautious."

"Well, it wasn't in his room, or in his suitcase."

"Have you looked in the hotel safe?" she asked. "Whenever he checked into a hotel, he always put his envelope in the hotel safe."

I dropped a five-dollar bill on the table and made for the door marked "Lobby." Barbara was close beside me.

Ten

"Christ," I breathed, dropping one blue-covered affidavit on the bed and reaching for another one. "It looks like your father had the goods."

She'd put on horn-rimmed glasses, and was rapidly riffling through several pages of legal-size, lined yellow paper. Each page was covered with Murdock's untidy scrawl. "He was right," she said softly. "It would've made a great story. It'll still make a great story."

Looking at the papers scattered across the bed, I said, "I wonder whether the murderer knew these notes existed."

She pushed the glasses up into her hair. "Why do you say that?"

"Because," I said slowly, thinking it out as I spoke, "if he was after the notes, then he would've—" I glanced at her apologetically before I said, "He would've tried to find out where the notes were hidden, before he killed your father."

"Maybe he did find out. "Maybe he—" She winced. "Maybe he forced Dad to tell him, before he killed him."

"I don't think so. If it had happened like that—if the murderer was primarily interested in the notes—then he wouldn't have killed your father. Not before he got the notes, anyhow. He'd have gotten the notes first, to guard against the possibility that your father lied to him."

She looked at me for a long, troubled moment, then asked, "What's going to happen to them?" She was sitting on one corner of the queen-size bed. She'd taken off her shoes and her jacket. I was aware that her silken blouse outlined small, perfectly proportioned breasts.

"Ultimately," I said, "it's a legal question. And I'm no lawyer. But it seems to me that for now, the state—the police—should take custody of them, as evidence. Eventually, as part of your father's estate, they'll go to you."

"If Sheppard gets to them long enough to make copies, though, they'd be worthless. Or, at least, they'd be debased."

"Sheppard claims they're his property," I answered. "If he knows they've been found, he'll hire lawyers. Lots of lawyers."

"I can hire lawyers, too."

"Not as many as Sheppard can hire."

"What about now?" she asked.

"What do you mean?"

"They're in your possession. Police possession. Is it possible that Sheppard could get to them—make copies of them?"

"That's another legal question. And it takes time to resolve legal questions—days, or weeks, or months. For now, though—for the next day or two—it's my decision. And I can tell you that I'm not going to let Sheppard get to them." As I spoke I was thinking of Avery Rich's dry, precise voice on the phone. Had he called the mayor? How long would it take for the mayor to call the police commissioner—for the commissioner to call Dwyer, the police chief?

"What if Sheppard demands to see them—just to read them, without copying them?"

"The same thing applies. As far as I'm concerned, these

notes and the affidavits are evidence in a homicide investigation. If the contents are made public too soon, the investigation might be compromised." I looked at her. "That applies to you, too—" I pointed to the pages she still held in her hands. "I don't know what you've been reading in those notes. But whatever it is, I want you to keep the contents to yourself."

"I knew you were going to say that."

"I mean it, Barbara." Again, I pointed to the sheaf of notes. "That's evidence. As such, it's police property. Police business."

"The murder of my father," she said slowly, "is my business." Her chin lifted; her small mouth settled into a firm, unyielding line. Her eyes came up, quietly challenging me. I could see both desperation and determination in her eyes—both dignity and despair. In that instant I thought I could see deep into the past, the present and the future of Barbara Murdock. I thought I could see a little girl who'd been too precocious, a young woman who could be too willful and, finally, an older woman who would be too lonely.

I could also see that she didn't intend to stand aside, waiting for someone else to find her father's murderer.

I moved around the foot of the bed and stood above her. She rose to face me, and for a moment we stood close together, silently confronting each other. I was aware that the rhythm of her breathing had quickened. Close to my chest, her breasts were rapidly rising and falling. In response, I felt my genitals tightening.

"His murder is my business, too," I said. "I'm on your side."

"I know that."

I put out my hand, palm up. "Give me the notes."

Without a word, she gathered the sheets of lined yellow paper together, folded them once and gave them to me.

"I've already read them, you know." She spoke quietly. Defiantly.

I drew a deep breath. "I'm telling you again. Don't talk about those notes. If you do—and if you foul up my investigation, you could be prosecuted." I stared at her for a long, hard moment before I added, "That's what I told Sheppard, too. I threatened to have him locked up if he didn't cooperate. I could do it, too."

"No," she answered. "No, you couldn't have Jeffrey Sheppard locked up. Never."

"We'll see."

She stepped away from me and pointed to the affidavits still scattered across the bed. "I don't know what you got from those, Lieutenant. But I can tell you what I got out of those—" She gestured to the sheets of yellow paper.

"So?"

"So I can tell you that you're dealing with a lot of very important people. They aren't the kind of people you can throw in the back of a police car and haul off to jail. If these people go to jail, they drive to the Hall of Justice in chauffeur-driven limousines, and they surrender in style. Then, an hour later, they're out on bail. Their chauffeurs don't even go home. They just wait at the curb."

"But, still, they go to jail."

Stubbornly, she shook her head. "No, they don't. I know how the system works. I know—and you know—that rich men don't go to jail."

"I don't agree. I've put a few rich people in jail. Not many, I admit. But a few. The more expensive their lawyers, the longer the process takes. But they still go to jail."

"Bullshit."

I shrugged.

Again, she pointed to the notes. "When you put Baxter Wardell in jail, I want to hear about it. I want to be the first to know."

Involuntarily, I looked down at the notes. "Baxter Wardell?" Asking the question, I struggled to put a person with the name—and couldn't. Yet, certainly, I'd heard the name.

"As you'll discover when you read Dad's notes," Barbara said, "the name of 'Wardell' keeps popping up. The notes are pretty cryptic, I'll admit. Dad always kept as much in his head as he kept on paper. And, in fact, he didn't mention 'Baxter' once. Just 'Wardell.' But I'm sure—dead sure—that somewhere in those affidavits, someone states that Baxter Wardell masterminded a multi-million-dollar arms swindle that involves the Pentagon. And a few assorted California congressmen. And, last but not least, a few assorted White House staffers."

I turned to the bed and began gathering the affidavits together. As I stuffed the salmon envelope full, and knotted the string, I asked, "Who's Baxter Wardell?"

"He's a wheeler-dealer," she answered. "A financier. Or a crook, take your pick. During the Second World War, his father made millions in scrap iron and real estate and God knows what else. At least once, I know, Wardell Senior was indicted for black-marketeering. But he never went to trial. After the war the old man began dealing in surplus munitions. Then Baxter Junior took over—fresh out of Harvard Business School. He became a munitions broker—among other things. Many, many other things, including international money manipulations. Did you read *The Silver Bears*, by any chance?"

"No."

"Well, it's all about men like Wardell. They're international currency speculators. Some of them are swindlers. But they score so big that they're above the law—because they control the politicians who make the laws. Except that you never hear about them. They pay people to keep their names out of the papers. Which is why you don't know anything about Wardell, for instance. Even though he lives in San Francisco."

"How do you know so much about Wardell?"

"Dad told me about him" she replied. Then, thoughtfully: "And now I know why."

"Why?"

"Because he was testing my reaction to Wardell's marketability," she answered promptly. "Market research."

"Did he tell you the rest of it—the munitions swindle at the Pentagon?"

"No."

"Are you sure?"

She eyed me for a frosty moment before she answered, "I'm sure, Lieutenant. That's the way Dad operated. He'd tell different people bits and pieces. He did it partly to test reactions—to see whether I, for instance, was interested in knowing about Wardell. But no one knew the whole story. Not until Dad was ready to break it. He—"

Beside the bed, the phone rang. Startled, she stepped quickly to the bedside table and snatched up the receiver. As she said "hello" I glanced at my watch. The time was almost eleven.

"Oh—yes," she was saying. "Just a moment, please." She handed the phone to me.

"This is Communications, Lieutenant. Allingham speaking."

"Hello, Allingham. What is it?"

"Lieutenant Friedman would like to talk to you. He's got some information on the Murdock homicide."

"Put him on."

Three clicks, and Friedman came on the line. "Are you interrogating the Murdock woman?" he asked. "Shall I call back?"

"It's all right. What've you got?"

"We just heard from the FBI in Washington on the prints from that compress wrapping," Friedman said. "It looks like we could've caught a big fish."

"Who?"

"The name is Joey Annunzio." Friedman paused, for the effect. "Ever hear of him?"

"No."

"Well, Joey Annunzio happens to be a highly respected hit man with many, many satisfied customers, mostly in the Mafia. Which explains the ice pick and the compress and all the other nice little professional touches that we admired so much."

"It makes sense."

"Also," Friedman said, "it just so happens that an FBI courier is flying out here tomorrow—to the San Francisco FBI office. And he's going to bring copies of the whole Annunzio file, including pictures. Which is a break."

Balancing the salmon envelope on my hand I said, "I've got something, too."

Friedman chuckled. "I can hear that laconic, Western-marshal note in your voice. Which is always a dead give-away. You've got a scoop. Right?"

"I might've found out why Murdock came to San Francisco."

"Are you coming down to the Hall?" he asked. Then: "Before you answer, I should mention that I was just going home to bed. You want to call me at home?"

"That's all right. It'll keep. I'm going home, too. I'll see you at the office tomorrow. Besides—" Smiling, I looked at Barbara. "Besides, the suspect I've turned up isn't going to start running."

"It sounds intriguing."

"It is."

"It also sounds like tomorrow could be a big day."

"It could be."

Eleven

"I was right," Friedman said. "Today could be a big day."
He gestured to the affidavits and the sheets of lined yellow
paper now stacked in piles on my desk. "Except that when
Chief Dwyer sees that stuff—especially the stuff about
Baxter Wardell—the chief is going to crap right in the seat
of his pin-striped trousers. I happen to know that Dwyer
suffered one loosening of the bowels already this morning,
when he heard from the commissioner, who'd heard from
Avery Rich, who'd just heard from Jeffrey Sheppard."

"I'm surprised that I haven't heard from Dwyer."

"You will, I'm sure. After he recovers his composure.
Then, when he discovers that Wardell has got to be interrogated—" Friedman smiled, smugly satisfied at the thought
of Dwyer's discomfort. "I just hope I'm there," he said,
"when Dwyer hears about it. He thinks of Wardell as his
buddy, you know." Now the smile mischievously widened.
"Me, too."

"You?"

He nodded. "Years ago—before your time—some nut
decided he was going to extort a million dollars from Wardell by threatening to kill him. I'd just made inspector, at

the time, and I was Wardell's bodyguard. Or, rather, I was *one* of his bodyguards. He had several. His own, and the city's." Unwrapping his first cigar of the day, Friedman said, "Chief Dwyer was the head bodyguard. Except that he was Captain Dwyer, then. Even in those days, though, it was obvious that Dwyer was destined to be Chief. Show Dwyer someone with money, or power, or both, and Dwyer starts kissing ass. He learned when he was a patrolman, and he never forgot. So, naturally, he started kissing Wardell's ass—with a passion."

I shook my head. "I don't understand how you ever made lieutenant," I said. "I really don't. You—Christ—you never miss a chance to take a crack at Dwyer, or the mayor, or the commissioner. Not to mention most of the captains and both deputy chiefs."

"The answer to the question is simple," he said. "It's possible—barely possible—to get as far as lieutenant purely on merit, without kissing ass. It doesn't happen often. But it does happen. It happened to me—and it happened to you, too. Of course, you had the advantage of looking like a lieutenant, which I never had. Still, we both made it with our virtue more or less intact. But lieutenant is as far as either of us is going."

"I don't agree."

"I know you don't. But that doesn't make me wrong. You wait. Ten years from now we'll both still be lieutenants. You think just because you're photogenic and show up on the six o'clock news sometimes that you're captain material. But you're wrong." He pointed his cigar at me. "You're too stubborn to make captain. And I'm too fat. Too fat, and too virtuous. Plus I'm Jewish, of course."

"Jewish doesn't count."

"No. But I'm a *smart* Jew. Too smart for my own good, promotionwise. I figured that out a long time ago. And you're too pigheaded, like I said."

"You've got a theory for everything, you know that?"

"That's because I'm a smart Jew. Like I said."

"Well, if you're so smart, what'd you suggest we do next?"

"I've got it all figured out—" He aimed his cigar at the notes and the affidavits. "First, we duck around the corner, and we make two Xeroxed copies of that stuff—one for me, and one for you. We return to the Hall, and we turn over the originals to the property room, after which we tell the D.A. we found the notes. Then we each take copies home. Just in case."

"You're saying that the originals could disappear."

Decisively, he nodded. "That's exactly what I'm saying. Either disappear, or get buried."

In silence, we stared at each other. It wasn't the first time we'd bent the rules. Slowly, somberly, I nodded. "All right. What else?"

"By that time," he said, "with luck, we'll have the FBI file on Annunzio. On the outside chance that Annunzio is still in town—which is less than fifty-fifty, I figure—we put Canelli and Culligan and about four other guys on Annunzio's trail, or the lack of it. Also, while we're at it, I think we should turn Richard Blake loose."

"He doesn't want to be turned loose. Not until we've found Ricco."

"I can see Blake's point. However, if we turn him loose, and skillfully stake him out, and then put out the word that he's loose, Ricco might come out from his hole long enough to take a crack at Blake. Or, who knows, there might still be a connection between Blake and Annunzio."

"What kind of a connection?"

"Money," Friedman answered promptly. "Maybe Annunzio still owes Blake some money. It would make sense, considering that the usual deal is half up front and half after the job is finished."

"The job wasn't finished, though."

"That wasn't Blake's fault. And besides, these Mafia types are very scrupulous about debts."

Doubtfully, I shook my head. "It sounds like wishful thinking, Pete. Besides, I promised to protect Blake, if he told me what I wanted to know."

"You will be protecting him. You'll just be protecting him at his place, not ours."

Giving in, I shrugged. "All right. But you've got to tell him that you pulled rank."

"Agreed."

"What then?"

"Then," he said, "we go look for Baxter Wardell, my old buddy. But we won't tell anybody we're going to look for him. We'll pull the plug. I've got my car. We'll take that."

"Why pull the plug?"

"If we don't pull the plug, we'll have Dwyer perspiring all over us, sure as hell. As only Dwyer can perspire."

As I gathered up Murdock's papers, I said, "I've been thinking about what you said—about us being promoted. And you know what I think?"

"What'd you think?"

"I think that you're the reason I won't get promoted. You and all these little wars you have going with the brass."

Grinning slyly, Friedman dropped his cigar butt in the ashtray and heaved himself to his feet. "Warfare purifies the breed."

"And saves the city the expense of pensions, sometimes."

"Touché."

Friedman set the handbrake and stared at a three-story brick town house. "It's the same place Wardell lived in when he was about to be assassinated," he said. "I'd've thought he would have moved up."

"How can you move up from a house like that?" I opened the car door and got out.

When Friedman joined me on the sidewalk I said, "According to Barbara, Wardell doesn't like publicity."

" 'Barbara,' eh?" Owlishly lecherous, Friedman leered at

me. "It's against regulations, you know, to screw around with witnesses."

"You didn't anwer the question."

"The answer is, yes, Wardell hates publicity. All crooks hate publicity."

"Why don't you take the lead, since you know him?"

"Right."

We swung open a tall iron gate and walked side by side to a pillared portico. The house was Georgian style, with fluted columns and intricate scroll trim accenting massive brick walls. Delicately segmented windowlights fanned above the stately front door. It was a house that should have been surrounded by acres of rolling lawns, with a circular driveway and stone lions guarding the entryway. I pressed the bell button and was adjusting my tie when the door swung open to reveal a Negro maid. She was dressed in the traditional servant's uniform: a small white cap, black organdy dress, white ruffled apron.

Feeling faintly foolish, I showed her my badge and asked to see Baxter Wardell.

"I'm sorry but Mr. Wardell isn't in. Can I help you?" As she spoke, she glanced again at the badge. Her expression was unreadable.

"Can you tell us where we could find him?" Friedman asked. "We have some important information for him. We've got to locate him as soon as possible."

She hesitated, then asked, "What kind of information?"

"Sorry—" Friedman smiled at her. "We'll have to talk to Mr. Wardell. It's got to do with one of his business enterprises. There's been an accident involving an associate of his. A serious accident."

Her calm, calculating gaze was plainly skeptical as she took a moment to look Friedman over. Like many blacks, she'd developed a finely tuned ear for a con.

"Just a minute, please." She began to close the door on us, then thought better of it. "Would you like to step in? I'll see if Mrs. Wardell's free."

100

"Thank you." We followed her into a high-ceilinged, walnut-paneled entry hall. Two carved chairs flanked a small Regency side table. Arranged in a blue-and-white Wedgewood vase, a bouquet of white carnations had been placed in the exact center of the table. The maid gestured us to the two chairs and disappeared down the hallway. Less than a minute later she reappeared, smiled perfunctorily and asked us to follow her. We walked on a succession of Oriental rugs to the rear of the house, where the maid gestured us through the open door of a sun room. One wall of the room, floor to ceiling, was glass, offering a spectacular view of the Golden Gate Bridge. In front of the glass wall, exotic splashy-leafed plants grew out of a huge fieldstone planter as wide as the wall. The floor was terrazzo, covered with woven wool rugs. The furniture was made of expensive walnut-stained rattan. With the exception of a huge abstract wall sculpture, the white-painted brick walls were bare.

Wearing a dark-gray flannel skirt and a tailored pink oxford-cloth shirt, a woman reclined in a chaise longue placed to face the glass wall. She was a small, compactly made woman of about forty. Her closely cut auburn hair was softly, deftly styled. Her features were delicately drawn on a classic oval face. Beneath gracefully arching brows, her eyes were a dark, vivid brown. It was a patrician face— a contessa's face.

While Friedman made the introductions and stated our business, I watched the woman's eyes for a reaction. I saw nothing. Both her body and her face were inert, utterly composed. She held a copy of a brightly jacketed novel in her lap. Using a tooled-leather bookmark, she marked her place, closed the book and put it on a small table beside the chaise. I noticed that the book, like the vase of flowers in the entryway, had been placed precisely in the center of the table. I heard her sigh faintly. Plainly, she regretted leaving the story.

"Would you like to sit down?" She gestured to a pair of

matching chairs. Her voice was soft and low-pitched, curiously uninflected. Her dark eyes still revealed nothing. When we'd seated ourselves, she simply looked at Friedman, waiting for him to begin. He repeated the same lie he'd told the maid, with embellishments. When he finished speaking, she looked at him for a long, inscrutable moment before she said, "I think Baxter got in yesterday from London. I'm not sure whether he's still in town. Usually, if he's in town, it's not for more than a day or two. Still, it's Friday. He might stay for the weekend."

"Does he—" I hesitated. "Does he live here?"

She transferred her unfathomable gaze to me. Another moment of empty silence passed before she said, "Baxter has an apartment at the City Club."

"Then he—doesn't live here."

"Sometimes he gives dinner parties here. That's all." She spoke in the same low, expressionless voice.

"You say you think your husband arrived in San Francisco yesterday. Now—" Friedman waved a deprecating hand. "Now, I don't mean to put you on the spot. But are you reasonably sure of his schedule? For instance, are you sure he arrived from London yesterday?"

As he asked the question, her unreadable eyes moved deliberately from me to Friedman. "Reasonably sure," she said.

"But not entirely sure."

"No, not entirely."

As if he'd been expecting the answer, Friedman nodded. Then, casually, he said, "Several years ago there was a death threat made against your husband. I was one of his bodyguards. Here—" He waved his hand. "In this house."

"How many years ago, Lieutenant?"

"Ten or twelve. Maybe more."

"Then I wouldn't remember. Baxter and I have only been married for five years."

Friedman didn't respond but instead allowed another long silence to fall. I knew why he'd done it. He wanted to discomfort the woman—wanted to force some flicker of reaction from her. Questioned by police, most people reveal uneasiness, or annoyance, or excitement, or outright hostility. Not Mrs. Wardell. Half reclining on the chaise, fingers interlaced across a smooth, flat stomach, she betrayed no emotion, no anxiety. She simply waited for the next question. Watching her, I found myself remembering the abused wives I'd interrogated during my years as a policeman. Like Mrs. Wardell, many of them were curiously passive, awaiting the pleasure of others. At first glance, they sometimes seemed serene: fulfilled, at peace. But the truth always showed deep in their eyes. They were women without hope.

Finally Friedman spoke. "Do you read the newspapers, Mrs. Wardell?"

She nodded—a single, grave, measured inclination of her classic head. "Yes."

"Have you read about the man who was killed Wednesday night in North Beach? Eliot Murdock?"

Again, she nodded. "Yes, I read about that."

"We have reason to believe that Mr. Murdock was an—associate of your husband's. We also believe that Mr. Murdock may have come to San Francisco to see your husband."

She didn't respond, either by word or gesture.

"Did you ever hear your husband mention Eliot Murdock?"

Now she shook her head in a single measured, mechanical arc. "No. Never." She allowed a moment to pass before she added tonelessly, "My husband has hundreds of associates."

"Does he have many friends?" I asked.

With the typical slow, deliberate movement of her head, she turned to me. She looked at me silently for a moment before she said, "No, I don't think my husband has any friends, Lieutenant. When he was younger, I think he had friends. But not now." As she spoke, she turned her head until she was staring at the Golden Gate Bridge and the low green hills of the Marin headlands, framed so spectacularly by the glass wall. I thought she was about to retreat inside herself—into some secret place where she fought for her own sanity. I exchanged a look with Friedman. He shrugged, raised his eyes helplessly toward the ceiling, then moved his head to the door. I nodded, and was about to rise when the woman spoke. "You're lying, aren't you?"

I exchanged another look with Friedman, who said, "What do you mean, Mrs. Wardell?"

"I mean that you're here because you suspect Baxter caused that man's death."

"Yes, Mrs. Wardell," Friedman answered steadily. "Yes, that's why we're here." He let a beat pass, then said, "But how did you know?"

"I didn't know. But I suspected."

"Why?" Friedman spoke very softly, very cautiously—as if he were afraid of jarring her out of a shallow trance. "How?"

"Because of the things you didn't say," she answered, still staring out through the glass wall. "And because men like Baxter make people die."

"Make people die?"

She nodded. "Yes." She sat silently for another moment before she said, "Some men succeed because they're stronger than other men—or smarter—or better. But Baxter succeeds because he's cruel. So people die, because of Baxter."

"What you're really saying," Friedman said, "is that your husband ruins other people. He might cause them to commit suicide, for instance."

"Yes." To herself, she nodded. "Yes, that's what I'm

104

saying. Baxter is like a—a sorcerer. He has a strange power over people. First he attracts people. Then he possesses them. And then, finally, he destroys them." She paused, then repeated, "He destroys them. Sometimes they don't know until Baxter tells them. And then it's too late." Again she paused, still gazing off across the Golden Gate. And then her mouth moved in a small, pensive smile. "I'm waiting for Baxter to tell me," she said softly. "I've been waiting for a long time." Her voice was eerily disembodied. Her eyes were round and wondering, as if she were seeing a vision.

Slowly, respectfully, Friedman rose to his feet. Speaking softly, as if we were at a graveside, we said goodbye.

Twelve

"Have you ever been in here?" Friedman asked.

"No."

"Someone told me once that, literally, you have to be worth a million dollars before the City Club even lets you fill out a membership application."

"I can believe it."

We were sitting in a small reception room that opened off the City Club's entry hall. With its dark wood paneling, lofty ceiling, high casement windows and somber paintings of stern-looking men, the reception room was almost a caricature of the ultra-exclusive men's club. It was an austere room, not a comfortable one. There were no magazines on the long refectory table, no books on the shelves. The room was furnished with only four chairs, each of them rigidly straight-backed. Plainly, visitors weren't meant to feel at home. The room was the City Club's version of a holding cell, reserved for nonmembers and other undesirables.

"What'd you think of Mrs. Wardell?" I asked.

"I think she's a very strange lady." As he spoke, Friedman extracted a cigar from an inside pocket. Then, as he was unwrapping the cigar he glanced at a small metal ashtray placed in the center of the refectory table. Hardly larger than a coaster, the ashtray was spotless. Grunting, Friedman rewrapped the cigar and returned it to his pocket. "I also think she's probably a little crazy," he added.

"I wonder whether she was crazy before she married Wardell."

"I doubt it. I think Mrs. Wardell is damaged goods. Badly damaged goods."

"I had the feeling that she hates him."

"I had the feeling that she's lost the capacity for hatred," Friedman said. "I don't think she's got the energy. I think she *had* the energy. But I don't think she's got it now."

"She said Wardell was a sorcerer. I wonder whether she really believes it."

"If she believes it," Friedman said, "it's because that's what Wardell wants her to believe. He "

The massive oak door suddenly swung open. A man stepped quickly into the room, swung the door closed, then stood with his back to the door, staring at us. His age was the middle fifties. His height was about six feet. He weighed about one hundred seventy-five. Wearing a belted, khaki bush jacket, brown whipcord trousers and wear-burnished Wellington boots, with a soft cotton shirt open at the throat, he could have been dressed for a high-style African safari. His body was trim and taut: broad-shouldered, narrow-waisted, long-legged. His face was an arresting study of strength and purpose, with a squared-off jaw, a straight-across mouth and a high-bridged Roman nose. Beneath the dark, bold arch of thick eyebrows, his eyes were a clear, cold gray. His hair was coarse and graying, and grew low across a broad forehead. He had the face of a centurion—and the eyes of a gunfighter.

"Hello, Mr. Wardell—" Friedman rose to his feet and extended his hand. "I'm Lieutenant Peter Friedman. Several years ago I worked as your bodyguard." Friedman's smile was uncharacteristically ingratiating. Frowning, Wardell looked thoughtfully at Friedman's face, then glanced down at the outstretched hand.

"Friedman, you say." With obvious disinterest, Wardell shook hands. "I'm afraid I don't remember."

I introduced myself but didn't offer my hand. I already knew that I didn't like Baxter Wardell. And during that first moment of quick, uncompromising appraisal, I knew he didn't like me either.

Still standing with his back to the door, Wardell looked inquiringly at Friedman. "What can I do for you, Lieutenant?" He spoke coldly, impersonally.

"Are you acquainted with Eliot Murdock?" Friedman asked. "The columnist?"

Wardell frowned, then nodded impatiently. "I remember him, yes. He did a Washington gossip column. Several years ago."

Friedman nodded in return. "Right. Did you know him personally? Or just by reputation?"

"Just by reputation."

"Did you know that Murdock died?"

"Recently, you mean?"

"Very recently."

"No, I didn't know. But I can't say that I'm really interested, if you want the truth. Why? What's it all about?" As he spoke, he glanced pointedly at his watch. Countering subtly, Friedman gestured to the elaborately carved straight-backed chairs. "Can we sit down for a few minutes, Mr. Wardell?"

Wardell's eyes narrowed as he studied Friedman. In that moment it seemed as if everything about Friedman's past, present and future was being assessed, analyzed and computed behind Wardell's clear gray eyes. Finally, with his decision made, he said, "It'll have to be a *very* few minutes, Lieutenant. I'm already behind schedule, I'm afraid." Wardell tossed a leather portfolio on the table and sat in the chair closest to the door. He moved gracefully and economically, utterly assured. Yet his movements, like his speech, seemed subtly calculated, as if he were programmed by the same internal computer that had just assessed Friedman.

"Eliot Murdock was killed the night before last, Mr. Wardell," I said. "Wednesday night. Here. In San Francisco."

Shifting his attention from Friedman, Wardell studied me for a brief, patronizing moment before he said, "I don't understand what Eliot Murdock's death has to do with me. And I must tell you that I don't have time for guessing games. You'll either have to come to the point, or else you'll have to excuse me."

"We're trying to find out who murdered him. To do that, we need a motive. We've discovered that Murdock had information relating to a—" I hesitated. I didn't want to reveal too much. And I didn't want to antagonize him, giving him an excuse for angrily breaking off the interrogation. "Murdock was investigating what could turn out to be a multimillion-dollar kickback scheme, Mr. Wardell," Friedman interposed smoothly. "We have his notes, and your name appeared in them. So we thought you might be able to help us put some of the pieces together."

The gunfighter's eyes shifted to Friedman. "I hope," Wardell said, "that you aren't suggesting I had any part in this so-called scheme, Lieutenant." He spoke softly—ominously.

Once more flashing his improbably ingratiating smile, Friedman spread his hands. "As Lieutenant Hastings says, we're interested in Murdock's murder, not his investigations. We have no way of knowing whether his facts were right or wrong. We're only trying to determine whether his facts, so called, could have been a motive for murder."

109

"What are these 'facts' he had?" Wardell accented the single word with scornful precision.

"They apparently involve Pentagon arms sales," Friedman answered. He paused, then added, "We understand that you've been involved in similar deals in the past. That's probably why Murdock had your name in his notes."

Surreptitiously, I glanced at Friedman. Did he know that Wardell had been involved in the past sale of arms? Or was he fishing? His poker-player's eyes revealed nothing. But, privately, I decided he was fishing.

Wardell rose to his feet, picked up his slim leather portfolio and stood looking down at Friedman. He allowed a moment of intimidating silence to pass. Then, speaking in an aloof voice, he said, "I've been involved in literally thousands of 'deals,' as you call them. Some of them I'm personally involved in. Others I simply finance, after my subordinates have checked out the numbers. So, to answer the question, I couldn't tell you whether I've ever been involved in the sale of surplus munitions—not without checking the records. And checking the records, Lieutenant, can be a long, time-consuming process." He let another supercilious moment pass, allowing us to consider the value of his time. Then, speaking in the same cool, contemptuous voice, he continued: "I can tell you, though, that people like Eliot Murdock have been harassing me for years. They're a built-in nuisance, like flies or mosquitoes. And they are, in fact, the reason I pay people—several people—to keep my name out of the newspapers." As he paused again, for emphasis, he looked from Friedman to me, then back to Friedman. Speaking with slow, bludgeoning emphasis, he said, "Eliot Murdock was a hack and a muckraker and a pimp. And I can give you my personal assurance that any exposé he contemplated doing on me was, at best, a flimsy tissue of lies with just enough truth sprinkled through to beat the libel laws. That's the way Murdock always operated. And I'm sure twelve years of alcoholic silence hadn't changed him." To signify that his remarks were concluded, and the subject closed, Wardell let another beat pass. Then, in a lighter, all-is-forgiven voice, he said, "And now, if you gentlemen will excuse me, I've got a date with a B-25."

Spontaneously surprised, Friedman looked up sharply. During World War II he'd been a pilot. "Did you say a B-25?"

Patronizingly, Wardell nodded. "That's right. It's a propeller-driven bomber."

"I know," Friedman answered, giving Wardell his full, frank attention. "I used to *fly* one, for God's sake."

Already half turned toward the door, Wardell turned back, for the first time facing Friedman squarely. "You did? Really?" Characteristically, his eyes narrowed suspiciously. "Where?"

"North Africa," Friedman answered. "And Europe, too, with the Eighth Air Force. In 'forty-four and 'forty-five, out of England."

"My God, I flew fighters out of England. I've got one of them, too. A P-51."

"You've got a P-51 *and* a B-25?" Friedman asked incredulously. Then, wonderingly, "My God."

Decisively, Wardell nodded. "I've had a P-51 for ten years. I bought it for ten thousand dollars. It's worth eight times that now. The B-25 I just got. I'm taking delivery on it now, in fact. Right now. At the Schellville airport." Watching the sudden animation in Wardell's eyes, hearing the lift in his voice, I could see two aspects of the same man in conflict: Wardell, the aviation enthusiast versus Wardell the overbearing financier, conditioned to keep everyone a haughty, self-protective arm's length away. Inevitably, the financier's persona prevailed. As I watched, his eyes chilled, his face tightened. His shoulders shifted arrogantly, conveying an aura of imperial impatience. The great world was calling.

"Do you keep the '51 at Schellville?" Friedman asked.

"No." Wardell answered shortly. "I have an eighty-acre tract up in Marin County, with an airstrip. That's where I keep the '51. I think I can use the strip for the B-25, too, if I fly it unloaded."

"How long is your airstrip?"

"Almost three thousand feet."

Friedman was about to respond, but Wardell curtly cut him off, nodded to me, and disappeared through the carved oak door.

"Jesus," Friedman said, staring at the closed door and shaking his head. "Jesus. A '51 and a B-25. I can't believe it."

"Did you really fly one in the war? A B-25?"

"Absolutely."

"How many engines does it have?"

"Two," he answered absently. Then: "My God, do you have any idea how much hundred octane gas it takes, just to get a B-25 off the ground?"

I didn't answer.

"I would like to see that airstrip," Friedman said. "I would *really* like to see that airstrip. I'll bet it's more like a private airport than an airstrip. I'll bet it's got a goddamn snack bar."

"For a minute or two," I said, "I thought he was going to turn into a human being, talking about airplanes."

Smiling, Friedman shook his head. "Not Baxter Wardell. Never Baxter Wardell. He's a complete, hundred and ten percent phony. If he ever allowed anyone to get to him, he'd shrivel up into a normal-size human being and promptly blow away."

"What'd you think of his answers?"

"I was interested," Friedman said thoughtfully. "I was very, very interested." As he said it, the old flyer's nostalgic light faded from his eyes, replaced by his customary on-the-job stare, impassively reflective. "Especially, I was in-

112

terested in the part where he was talking about the exposé Murdock was doing on him—considering that neither one of us said anything about an exposé."

"And also considering that Murdock was apparently trying to keep the story under wraps until it broke. Even his own daughter didn't know that Wardell was involved. Or his editor, either."

"Exactly," Friedman said. We were both standing, staring abstractedly at each other as we tried to fix the details of the brief interrogation in our memories. Finally Friedman smiled—his habitually sly, smug, cat-and-mouse grin. He'd thought of something—some subtle angle, some small wedge. Some special twist that appealed to him.

"Well?" I asked, watching him. "What?"

"I was just thinking," he said softly, "that it would be wonderfully ironic if it turned out that Baxter Wardell, international financier and playmate of presidents, made the same mistake that most petty hoods make -and just plain talked too much, trying to get himself off the hook."

"I was thinking the same thing," I said, nodding. "The very same thing."

"I was thinking something else," Friedman said musingly.

"What's that?"

"I was thinking," he said, "that if Wardell tries to take a B-25 off a runway that isn't at least five thousand feet long, it won't make much difference whether he's conning us or not."

Thirteen

Friedman had parked the family Ford in the City Club's passenger zone, and we drove off under the disapproving stare of a uniformed doorman.

"It's always amazed me," Friedman said, "how the servants of the very rich acquire their employers' snobbish bad manners." He pointed to the doorman. "Can you imagine what happens to him after he takes off his admiral's uniform and goes home to his overweight wife and underweight kids?"

I gestured to a police call box on the next corner. "Why don't I call in?"

"Good idea." He stopped the car beside the box and turned on the radio, trying to find a local newscast.

Communications had an urgent message for me to call Canelli. Less than a minute later Canelli came on the line. "I been trying to get through to you for about fifteen minutes," he said. "Or maybe twenty. I couldn't find Lieutenant Friedman either."

"What've you got?"

"Well," Canelli said, "I think we might have a break on Annunzio, Lieutenant. And all it took me was about a half hour on the phone, if you can believe it."

"Try me."

"What happened," Canelli said, "was that I decided, what the hell, I'd check the rent-a-car concessions at the airport for Wednesday, which was the day I figured he probably came in. Of course, we already checked the incoming flight for Annunzios, and Thorsons, and everything. But I figured he could always give the airline a phony name. To rent a car, though he'd have to show a driver's license, and everything. So I called them. And, would you believe it, I connected first time out." I heard paper rustle. "Joseph Annunzio, from Miami. Arrived Wednesday afternoon, which would be about right."

"Is the car still checked out?"

"Yes, sir," he said. "I just called the agency to verify it. Just a few minutes ago. And it's still out."

"What've you done about it?"

"Put out an APB," he answered promptly. "Also, right now, we're calling all the motor hotels and all the downtown parking garages, giving them the description of the car, and the license number, and all that."

"Good, Canelli. It sounds like a break."

"I also got the car agency staked out, in case he brings it back."

"Good."

"I was surprised that he's still around. I mean, I thought he'd've left town, after the job."

"Maybe he's got some unfinished business," I said.

"Or maybe he's sticking around to do some sightseeing."

"Maybe," I answered doubtfully. "Is there anything else?"

"Not really, Lieutenant. We're checking out Walter Frazer, but so far we got nothing that says he's not just a well-heeled lawyer who had his car stolen."

"Well, keep on it. What about Blake?"

"He's gone home, about two hours ago. I had someone pick him up at the hospital and take him to his apartment."

"Have you got him staked out?" I asked sharply.

"Yes, sir. I put two teams on it. Lieutenant Friedman's orders."

Relieved, I nodded at the phone. "That's right. Good." As I spoke I heard a buzzer sound three times, urgently. It was the "hotshot" signal. Canelli had an important call.

"Hey, I got a hotshot, Lieutenant. Want to hold on, or should I call you back?"

"I'll hold on."

I heard a click, then silence. I turned to Friedman, holding up one finger. Listening to the car radio, he nodded indifferently. Less than a minute later, Canelli's voice came back on the line: "Hey, Lieutenant," he said excitedly. "It happened. Jesus, I can't believe it."

"*What* happened?"

"We got Annunzio located. He's registered under the name of Thompson at the Beakman Motor Inn, on Van Ness. Both the make of the car and the license plate check."

"Is he at the Beakman now? On the premises?"

"I don't know, Lieutenant. The car's there, though."

"We're less than five minutes from the Beakman. We'll park around the corner, on Pacific, or Jackson, whichever it is. Get three men, and meet us there. Make sure everyone has walkie-talkies. We"ll need a couple of shotguns, too. Clear?"

"Yes, sir. That's clear."

Except for a chambermaid trudging sore-footed behind her linen cart, the corridor was deserted. I waited until the maid turned the corner, then raised my walkie-talkie.

"This is position one. All set?"

"Position two is ready," Friedman answered. With Culligan, Friedman was concealed on one of the two outside balconies that flanked Annunzio's balcony. Both Friedman and Culligan carried shotguns. Canelli and I, in the hall-

116

way, carried revolvers. Two detectives from General Works were in the garage downstairs, watching Annunzio's rented Oldsmobile. In constant contact with both our walkie-talkie net and Communications, the two G.W. men were our reserve unit. Friedman had located a small stepladder. When Canelli and I were inside Annunzio's room, Friedman and Culligan would climb the ladder and drop down into Annunzio's balcony. When he'd proposed the plan, I'd wondered aloud whether Friedman could drop over a six-foot wall without hurting himself. He'd been offended.

"How's it look back there? I asked. "Can you see into his room?"

"No," Friedman answered. "There's a sliding glass door, but the drapes are drawn."

"Are you ready?"

"We're ready."

"All right. We're going in."

"Right."

So that Friedman could hear us, I slipped my walkie-talkie into its case at my belt, switched on. I drew my revolver, nodding for Canelli to do the same. "I'll go in low," I whispered, "and break to the right. You break to the left. Clear?"

"That's clear," Canelli breathed.

"Okay. Let's do it." With my revolver clamped under my left arm, I slipped a passkey into the lock and slowly, cautiously turned the knob. When the door came open a quarter of an inch, I dropped the key into my pocket, took my revolver in my right hand and used my left hand to inch the door past the point where a night chain would hold it. Then, suddenly, I banged open the door. Bent double, I cleared the doorway and broke to my right, fast. Close behind me, breathing noisily, Canelli lunged into the room to find cover behind a gold-brocaded armchair.

117

The room was empty.

The double bed's elaborately quilted bedspread was unwrinkled. Even before we searched the closet and the dresser drawers, I sensed that Annunzio was gone and wouldn't be back.

Outside the sliding glass door, feet thudded heavily on a concrete slab. The door rattled as someone jerked at the handle, hard.

"Never mind," I called. "He's gone."

Automatically, by the book, Canelli and I quickly team-searched the closet and the bathroom. The closet was empty; the bathroom obviously hadn't been touched since the maid left. Dresser drawers and the medicine cabinet yielded nothing. Holstering my revolver, I stepped to the sliding doors, drew back the floor-to-ceiling drapes and flipped the lock. Cradling their shotguns in the crooks of their arms, Friedman and Culligan strode casually into the room. In due time, I thought, incidentally, the departmental comptroller's office would charge yet another fruitless search-and-secure mission against Homicide.

"Don't touch anything," I ordered needlessly. And to Canelli, "Let's get a fingerprint team up here."

"Yes, sir." Holstering his revolver and taking out his handkerchief, Canelli reached for the phone. While he dialed, Friedman and I stepped aside.

"Don't take it so hard," he said dryly. "Just the other day I read that a little adrenaline kick is good for the heart, once in a while." He emptied his shotgun, took the required "safety click" and tossed the gun on the bed.

Ruefully, I snorted—then remembered to switch off my walkie-talkie.

"What now?" he asked.

"How the hell should I know?" I retorted.

"Maybe," he said mildly, "I should go back to the Hall. You and Canelli can stay here, and find out when and how Annunzio left. Meanwhile, I'll make sure the airport guards have Annunzio's description."

"All right."

While we'd been talking, Canelli had come to stand a respectful three paces away, apologetically clearing his throat.

"What is it, Canelli?" I asked irritably.

"Well, ah, I've got a message from Chief Dwyer's office for you, Lieutenant."

Exchanging a resigned look with Friedman, I turned to face Canelli fully. "What's the message?"

"As soon as either you or Lieutenant Friedman get back to the Hall, you're supposed to report to the Chief. It's, ah—" He cleared his throat again. "It's got something to do with Jeffrey Sheppard, and Murdock's notes, or something. The way I get it, Sheppard's down at the Hall. And he's raising hell."

Trying to put the ball in his court, I exchanged a questioning glance with Friedman. "I'll handle Sheppard," he said airily. "And Dwyer, too. No sweat." Taking his shotgun from the bed and beckoning for Culligan to follow, he strode out through the open door, flipping his hand back over his shoulder. With the shotgun tucked under his arm, he looked like a jaunty hunter, off for a carefree pheasant hunt.

Fourteen

After interrogating a half-dozen motel employees, Canelli and I determined that Annunzio had surreptitiously left the motel early that morning, probably before eight o'clock. During his two nights at the Beakman, Annunzio had been a quiet, unobtrusive guest. He'd arrived Wednesday at four P.M. and had paid cash for three nights' lodging. The maid testified that he'd been traveling light, with only one medium-sized suitcase that he'd always kept closed and locked. He'd made no phone calls through the switchboard, either local or long distance. The garage attendant only remembered his driving the rental Olds once, on Thursday. The motel manager remembered that shortly after Annunzio arrived on Wednesday, he made several phone calls from the public booth in the lobby, once asking the manager for change—dimes and quarters. A check of the car-rental agency revealed that the Olds had been rented with a Master Charge card issued to Joseph Annunzio, of Miami Beach.

Canelli and I were drinking coffee in the motel's coffee shop when the pager clipped to my belt buzzed, and Communications asked me to phone Friedman at the Hall.

"I just finished talking with Dwyer," Friedman said heavily.

To myself, I smiled. "It sounds like you came out second best."

"I'll settle for a draw."

"What happened?"

"What happened," Friedman said, "is that Dwyer's crapping in his pants. And the odor is going to get worse, not better."

"What about Murdock's notes? Is Dwyer going to give them to Sheppard?"

"He's 'taking it under advisement,'" Friedman mimicked savagely. "He said he wanted my 'input,' before he decides. Which, translated, means that Dwyer wants me for a pigeon if Sheppard fouls up our chain of evidence."

"What'd you say?"

"I said he could go screw himself. Politely, of course. I said that he should let the city attorney decide the merits of Sheppard's claim. By the time we get a decision from the C.A., I figure we might have someone in custody."

"Good. You did just right."

"Don't sound so smug. It'll be your turn next. As soon as you show up here, he's going to want your 'input,' sure as hell. Christ," he grated, "I can't stand these prissy-assed, pseudo-intellectual catch phrases."

"What'd he say about the Wardell interrogation?"

"Nothing."

"Nothing?"

"He didn't say anything," Friedman explained, "because I, ah, didn't get a chance to mention that we talked to Wardell."

"What?"

"That's one of the reasons I'm calling," he said blandly. "I wanted to tell you not to blow the whistle on me. Wardellwise, that is."

"Listen, Pete—" I paused, considering how to put it. "I

don't mind all these private little war games you play with Dwyer, and the mayor, and assorted other politicians. I enjoy them, in fact. And I admire you for your principles. And most of the time I agree with what you're doing, and go along with you. But—" Again, I hesitated. "But I don't want you to include me in. Not automatically, anyhow. Not without checking with me first. Already, we've taken private possession of evidence—the notes. Fine. I agreed to it. You propositioned me, and I agreed. But when you tell Dwyer we didn't interview Wardell, you're putting me in the middle. You're—"

"I didn't deny that we interviewed him. I just didn't mention it."

"It's the same thing," I answered quietly. "And you know it. Right now—right this minute—Wardell's lawyers could be knocking on Dwyer's door. And when he discovers that we interrogated Wardell, and didn't tell him about it, he's *really* going to crap in his pants."

"I've considered all that," he answered airily. "And it's no problem. The way the conversation went, Dwyer was so steamed up about Sheppard and Avery Rich and the power of the press and the damage this case could do to his career that I didn't get in more than a few words. It was his fault that he didn't hear about Wardell. Not my fault."

"Bullshit."

"However," he continued, "to cover our asses I've written up a report on the Wardell interrogation and put it in channels. If Dwyer doesn't read the report, he's got only himself to blame."

I paused again. Then, deliberately pitching my voice to a hard, uncompromising note, I said, "You didn't listen. I'm trying to tell you that I don't want you deciding when I need my ass covered."

A moment of tight silence passed before he said, "I'm listening. And, what's more, I'm agreeing with you. You're right. I was wrong." He spoke slowly, in a low, reluctant monotone.

I realized that I was holding the phone away from my face, incredulously staring at it. Finally: "In all the years I've known you," I said, "that's the first time I've ever heard you admit that you're wrong."

"That's because I've never been wrong before." Now he was speaking in his normal voice—casually, irreverently.

"Oh." Glad of the chance to ease the tension, I spoke with broad sarcasm. "That explains it." I realized that I was smiling.

"Incidentally, Dwyer has something else on his mind, besides the missing notes. He thinks we made a mistake, turning Blake loose. He wants us to pick him up again and hold him as a material witness."

"Why?"

"He's afraid that Annunzio might get to him."

"He could be right. We were thinking about collaring Ricco when we turned Blake loose. But with Annunzio still in town, I think Dwyer's right."

"Maybe so," Friedman said grudgingly. "Why don't you and Canelli pick Blake up?"

"We're on our way."

"There it is," Canelli said, pointing. "Three eighty-seven Mason Street. He lives on the top floor."

It was a typical Tenderloin apartment building. Originally built in the twenties to offer luxury apartments close to the center of town, the building was now plainly infected by urban blight. A motley assortment of bedsheets, cheap bamboo blinds and torn lace curtains fluttered in its windows. Wooden boxes tacked to crumbling window sills served as makeshift refrigerators. Only the building's massive brick-and-stone construction had saved it from decay and ultimate destruction. It was a four-story building, with an all-night grocery and a pornographic bookstore occupying the ground floor.

I glanced at my watch. The time was four o'clock. The

weather had turned cold and raw. Over the ocean to the west, dark clouds lay heavily on a purple horizon. By morning the season's first rains were predicted.

"Where's the surveillance team?" I asked.

"I don't know, Lieutenant. I sent Marsten and Swig out. I didn't go with them."

"Well, it doesn't matter. We can—"

"There's Swig—" Canelli interrupted. "Over there, in that green Ford. In front of the topless bar." As Canelli spoke, Swig sat up straighter in his seat, furtively waving. I lifted four fingers, then switched on my mini walkie-talkie and turned the channel selector to four.

"Anything?" I asked, leaning to my left, to conceal the radio behind the dashboard.

"Nothing."

"Where's Marsten?"

"He's out in back. In the alley."

"Find out if he's seen anything."

"Yes, sir."

A moment later Swig came back on the air. "Marsten says that about fifteen minutes ago the subject went up on the roof of the building. He took the fire escape up, Marsten says. He was wearing a sweat shirt and clogs, and had a towel under his arm."

I looked up at the building's roof. On the left, 387 Mason Street shared a common wall with a taller building, six stories high. The building on the right was the same height as 387 Mason, but the two buildings were separated by at least ten feet. If, for some reason, Blake decided to run, escape across the rooftops was impossible.

"All right. We've come to take him into custody. Advise Marsten. Hold your positions until we've got Blake in the car. Then you can take off. The surveillance is over."

"Right."

As we got out of the car and walked across the narrow, littered street, Canelli said, "It sounds like Blake's taking a

124

sun bath." He looked up at the sky. "It's sure not much of a day for it."

Not replying, I pushed open the sagging door and crossed the lobby to the stairs. "No elevator," Canelli muttered. "Naturally."

Five minutes of hard, sweaty climbing took us to the fourth-floor corridor, where we stopped to catch our breath. The foul-smelling corridor reeked of stale cooking, urine and dust. As we stood panting, a door opened. A tall, blond man dressed in tight leather trousers and a purple velour shirt stepped out into the hallway. He wore his bleached shoulder-length hair in Shirley Temple ringlets; tiny diamonds sparkled in his ear lobes. He took two steps toward us, hesitated, then turned his back on us. Twitching his hips, he returned to his room. A moment later I heard a night chain rattle.

"There's the fire escape." Canelli pointed to a red "Exit" sign at the end of the corridor.

The rusty, iron fire escape creaked and rattled as we climbed up to the roof and over a carved stone parapet. Blake was lying on a brightly striped beach towel spread out on the tar-and-gravel roof. He was stripped to the waist, displaying a narrow-chested, rib-slatted torso. A blue sweat shirt was folded to pillow his head. A half-empty pint of Southern Comfort lay on its side, close to Blake's hand. His eyes were closed. Like a corpse laid at rest, his hands were crossed across his chest.

In the street below, the wail of an ambulance siren had covered the sound of our arrival. Now, suddenly, the shriek of the siren died.

"Blake."

The muscles of his naked chest convulsed. On its scrawny neck his head jerked spasmodically toward the sound of my voice. His right hand darted down to his blind side—going for a gun.

In the same instant that I dropped into a crouch, drawing my revolver, I saw recognition flash in his face—followed by pop-eyed, slack-jawed relief.

"Oh—Jesus—Lieutenant." He looked at me, looked at Canelli, then looked down at the chrome-steel Saturday-night special in his hand. He blinked at the gun, frowned, shook his head. Even before he spoke I knew instinctively what he'd say, and how he'd say it: "I—just—just happened to find it here. Honest. Someone just—just—" Still frowning earnestly, he continued to stare at the gun. Then, carefully, he placed it on the towel beside the half-filled bottle of Southern Comfort. "I guess maybe somebody ditched it up here, probably."

"I guess so." I holstered my revolver, walked across the graveled rooftop and picked up the gun. Realizing that the situation offered me a chance to reestablish my credibility with Blake, I emptied the small chrome-plated .22 revolver and dropped the gun and cartridges into my pocket. "Some hood ditched it, probably."

"Or some dope pusher, maybe," Canelli said, straight-faced.

Blake suddenly sat up on the beach towel. Avoiding our eyes, he unfolded his sweat shirt and slipped it over his shoulders. Goose pimples covered his stringy arms; he was shivering.

"It's cold," he muttered. "It got cold, all of a sudden."

"How come you're sunbathing today?" Canelli asked amiably. "There's hardly any sun."

Blake picked up the bottle of Southern Comfort and studied it for a moment. Finally he raised the bottle to me. It was a tentative, questioning gesture. "Do you, ah, mind if I have a little?"

"Go ahead."

Noisily, he gulped down most of the syrupy liquor.

"Ah—Jesus." He wiped his mouth and carefully recapped the bottle. "Jesus, that's good. See, I got this compulsion, I guess you'd call it. Whenever I'm locked up, even if it's just overnight, I start thinking about Southern Comfort. And I got to get out in the sun, too. Even if there isn't any sun. I still got to—" He let his voice die. Then, shivering and shaking his head, he said, "It's crazy, I guess. Like I said, it's a compulsion. A real hang-up." As he spoke he was looking at me, anxiously blinking his washed-out loser's eyes. "What about Ricco, Lieutenant?" he asked. "You found him yet?"

"We're working on it, Blake."

"Yeah. Well—" He licked his lips. "Well, I got an idea for you. I just thought about it. Just while I was lying here. I was going to give you a call, as a matter of fact."

"What's the idea?"

"Ricco owns a piece of a bar out on Mission Street. It's called the Wayfarer. It's not much of a bar—just one of those flea-bitten little neighborhood places. But I remember that once before, when he was hiding, he stayed in a room that's behind the bar. So maybe he's there. I mean, if you tried everywhere else, maybe he's there."

"We'll give it a try. Thanks."

"Yeah. Well, let me know."

"We will."

"Yeah. Well—" He got to his feet, placed the bottle of Southern Comfort on the gravel and began shaking out the beach towel. "Well, I guess I better get downstairs."

I waited for him to fold the beach towel and tuck it under his arm before I said, "We've got some news for you, Blake."

"News?" Anxiously scanning my face, he swallowed— once, twice. "What kind of news?"

"We've identified 'Thorson.' We know who he is."

"Who is he?"

"His name is Joey Annunzio."

"Wh—" The tip of his tongue circled his pale lips. "Who's Joey Annunzio?"

127

"Joey Annunzio is a professional hit man," Canelli said. "He's a heavyweight. A real heavyweight. He comes from Miami. That's where all the Mafia big shots are, you know. Miami."

"And he's still in San Francisco," I said.

"Cleaning up after himself, maybe," Canelli added. "Joey's very careful. Very tidy. He never leaves any loose ends."

"Jesus. I—"

"Did Ricco ever mention the name Annunzio to you?" I asked. "Ever?"

"No. Jesus. Never. I swear to God, he—"

"How about Thompson?" Canelli asked. "Did Ricco ever talk about Thompson?"

Blake was vehemently shaking his head. "No. No Thompson. Just Thorson. I swear to God, that's the only name I ever heard. Just Thorson." Clutching the beach towel and Southern Comfort bottle close to his scrawny chest, Blake turned to me. His eyes were round and virtuous, pleading with me as he began to whine: "Listen, Lieutenant, you gotta give me protection. I—Jesus—I trusted you. I did everything you said. *Everything*."

"While you were going to the Beresford with Thorson," I said, "did he say anything about how he got the Buick?"

"No. He just said that it was cool. I remember that. I asked him if he'd stolen it. And he said—"

From my left I heard the angry crack of a high-powered rifle. One shot—two—three. Canelli was yelling indignantly. Blake screamed. Something stung my face—brick chips, from a chimney. Momentarily I stood helplessly exposed, legs locked, arms useless. Then, slow-motion, I was throwing myself flat on the graveled roof. As I fell I twisted toward Blake. I saw his mouth come open. His round, anxious eyes blinked once—then froze in their sockets. Still clutching the bottle and the towel, he exhaled gently as his knees began to buckle. Slowly, reluctantly, he sank to an

128

awkward sitting posture—then suddenly fell hard on his side. The bottle bounced on the gravel and spun in a lazy half-circle. As the towel fell away from his chest, I saw a circle of blood centered on his heart.

Crawling awkwardly on elbows and knees, with his revolver in his right hand, Canelli was making for the stone parapet. Lying flat on my back, I fumbled for my walkie-talkie.

"*Swig.*"

"We heard it."

"He's on the roof to your left—the roof that's the same height as this one. Cover the front and back, you and Marsten. And get reinforcements, for God's sake. We'll stay here. Right here." I realized that I was ineffectually shouting. With great effort, I steadied my voice: "Do you read me?"

"Yes, sir. Roger."

I thrust the walkie-talkie in its case, drew my revolver and crawled across the rough gravel to crouch behind the parapet. Bent double, exposing only the top of his head, Canelli was staring at the neighboring roof, ten feet away.

"See anything?"

"When he first fired, before I dropped, I saw a head and a rifle," Canelli breathed. "He was crouched down like we are now, resting his rifle on the ledge."

Sitting flat, with my back against the parapet, I spoke into the walkie-talkie: "Swig?"

"Yes, sir."

"Have you got the front and back covered?"

"Yeah." As he spoke I heard a close-by siren. To myself, I nodded. The response time had been no more than a minute. Other sirens were coming, fast. In the Tenderloin cops were always close by.

"What kind of a building is it?" I asked.

"Apartments and ground-floor storefronts," Swig said. "Just like Blake's building."

"I want you and Marsten to seal the exits. Don't let anyone in or out. Tenants, customers—I don't care. No one leaves. Clear?"

"Yes, sir, that's clear."

"Has anyone come out of the front?"

A moment's hesitation. Then: "I don't think so. I had radio trouble for a few seconds. There was a lot happening. But I don't think anyone came out."

"We'll be down in a couple of minutes."

"Yes, sir."

I slipped the walkie-talkie in its case, twisted, rose to my knees and peered cautiously over the stone parapet. Then I glanced at the fire escape, twenty-five feet away. My suit was less than a year old, one of my favorites. I wasn't going to crawl on my hand and knees across twenty-five feet of gravel. "See anything, Canelli?" I asked.

"No, sir. He's gone down off the roof, probably."

"Let's stand up. We'll have a better angle."

"Right."

In unison, revolvers held ready, we straightened.

"Hey—" Canelli was pointing. "Look. There. By that door, there."

In its own small square enclosure, the door that led down from the roof was ajar. On the gravel beside the door I saw a rifle—a carbine, with a shortened barrel. Its wooden stock had been cut off just behind the bulge of the pistol grip.

"He's gone, sure as hell," Canelli said.

I holstered my revolver and turned to look at Blake. His sightless eyes were wide, staring up at the sky. His blue sweat shirt was blood-soaked.

"He was dead before he hit the ground," I said.

"Poor guy," Canelli said. "He was a loser. A real loser. I bet he hasn't laughed for ten years."

130

Fifteen

"What I can't figure out," Canelli said, "is how he got away so quick. I mean, that whole building was bottled up in two minutes. Less than two minutes."

I pointed to the next corner. "That's Twenty-ninth Street. It's not far, now."

"Right."

Bound for Ricco's Wayfarer bar, we were traveling south on Mission Street. The hour was six o'clock, dinner time. As we passed a Mexican restaurant I remembered that I hadn't eaten since breakfast.

"I wonder if he knew we were cops," Canelli mused.

"Who?"

"Annunzio."

"How do you know it was Annunzio?"

"Well, I—" He glanced at me, frowning. "I just think so. I mean, it looked like a professional hit. Don't you think so?"

Wearily, I nodded. "Yes, I think so." I was trying not to imagine what Dwyer would say, learning that Blake had been killed while he was talking to me. As soon as the building next to 387 Mason had been secured and a floor-by-floor, room-by-room search organized, I'd phoned Friedman at the Hall. When I finished my brief report there was a long silence on the line. Finally Friedman had sighed: a long, rueful exhalation.

"Earlier today you mentioned my war with the brass," he'd said. "I guess you know this is a major victory for the other side."

Already feeling angry and frustrated, suffering from the delayed shock of facing a gun, I'd sharply reminded him that releasing Blake had been his idea, not mine. And immediately I'd regretted saying it. "Sorry," I'd muttered. Then, trying to explain: "I tore my sleeve, crawling across the goddamn roof."

He'd sighed again. "Don't mention it. What about Ricco?"

I'd told him that Canelli and I were already in the Mission District, following Blake's tip.

"There it is," Canelli said. "The Wayfarer."

I'd phoned for reinforcements, and asked Culligan to set up operations at the scene. When we saw Culligan's empty cruiser parked in front of the Wayfarer, Canelli and I locked our own cruiser and walked inside. The Wayfarer was dark and dingy, barely wide enough to accommodate a red Formica bar and a single row of plastic-covered red barstools, many of them cracked across the seat. Behind the bar a mirror covered the entire wall. The mirror was garishly decorated with palm trees, rolling surf, sandy beaches and hula girls. Green plastic palm fronds and woven rattan mats were tacked to the walls. The Wayfarer smelled of dust, dampness and stale beer.

Culligan sat at one end of the bar; a General Works detective sat at the other end. Midway between the two detectives the bartender stood, leaning against the back bar, arms folded impassively across his Hawaiian shirt.

When Culligan saw us he unfolded his long, loose-limbed body, turned his back on the bartender and came to meet us. At the far end of the bar the G.W. man gestured for the bartender to join him, so that our conversation wouldn't be overheard. Culligan glanced back at the bartender, then spoke in a low voice. "It looks like an easy one, Lieutenant. All we do is go out through the back of the bar. There's an areaway back there, for garbage cans. The door to the apartment opens off the areaway. It's actually a separate little cottage. There's no rear entrance to the apartment. The only way out is two windows. But they're small, and they're about six feet high. Two G.W. guys are back there. There's a utility door that opens from the areaway to the sidewalk. It's bolted from the inside. Or, at least it was. I've got two uniformed men watching it. They're in a black-and-white car." Speaking in his customary slow, uninflected monotone, Culligan could have been repeating a shopping list. Now, with his report complete he stood with shoulders slumped, arms dangling slack at his sides. In the momentary silence I could hear his stomach rumbling. Culligan suffered from ulcers.

"What about Ricco? Have you seen him?"

"No. He got here three, four hours ago—about three o'clock, the bartender says. He hasn't come out since. The bartender says he came in with a woman. So the bartender figures—" Culligan hesitated. "He figures they're asleep by now. I went out there a couple of minutes ago, to try and see inside. But I couldn't. The shades were drawn."

I glanced over his shoulder. "How reliable is the bartender?"

Shrugging his bony shoulders, Culligan shook his head. "Beats me, Lieutenant." Culligan was always reluctant to commit himself.

"Guess."

Again he shrugged. "Probably reliable," he said grudgingly.

"Are the lights on in the apartment?" I asked.

"No."

"All right. The two of you stay here, on reserve. Canelli and I will go in. Tell the men outside. And close that—" I pointed to the front door. "We don't need spectators."

"Yes, sir." Culligan strode to the door, shot the bolt, then spoke into his walkie-talkie. I led the way down the row of barstools to the rear door. A short hallway with "his" and "hers" doors led to a big metal fire door, unbarred. I swung the heavy door back toward me and left it open. The cool night air was heavily laden with the smell of garbage. An oblong of light from the doorway fell on three rats working methodically at an overflowing refuse can. As I advanced, the rats moved reluctantly behind the cans.

I stepped to the service door that led to the sidewalk, verified that it was bolted, then walked to the door of the apartment. With my revolver drawn I stood silently for a moment, listening. Except for the scurrying sound of the rats I heard nothing. I reached cautiously for the doorknob—and touched freshly splintered wood. The door had been forced. It was closed but not latched. I flattened myself against the wall to the right of the door, then waited for Canelli to move to the left. Simultaneously, we nodded. I placed my fingertips against the door, and gently pushed. Creaking, the door swung open.

From inside, mingled with the fetid odor of garbage from the open areaway, I caught the unmistakable stench of violent death: vomit and excrement mixed with the sickly-sweet smell of drying blood.

Crouched over my revolver, I moved through the open doorway and into the darkened room. Pale light from a nearby street lamp filtered through two small windows set high in the rear wall. The twin shafts of light fell across a studio couch, opened into a double bed. A man and a woman lay side by side in the middle of the bed. Both were naked. Both had apparently been shot twice—once in the chest, once in the center of the forehead.

Instinctively, I'd been standing bent low over my revolver, straining against some unseen danger. Now, slowly, I straightened, holstered my revolver and stepped closer to the cool air coming through the open door.

"This one is yours, Canelli," I said. "I'm going to have dinner, and go home. Then I'm going to take a shower and put on my pajamas and bathrobe, and watch TV. When you've got it sorted out, you can call me. But not after eleven."

I'd just turned the channel selector for the eleven o'clock news when the phone rang.

"It's Canelli, Lieutenant. I meant to call you before this, but I've been bogged down. I mean, *really* bogged down."

"Bogged down?"

"Right," he answered fervently. "Bogged down. In about a hundred little pissy-assed details and complaints and God knows *what* all. Honest to God, Lieutenant, I don't know how you do it. Keep track of everything, I mean, and answer questions, and still not blow your stack. Especially at reporters."

"It's what Lieutenant Friedman calls the 'gift of command,' "I answered dryly. "What've you got?"

"Well, I got a couple of things, I guess. But, Jeeze, when I think of all the crap I put up with, trying to keep everything on track here, I—"

"Canelli. Please. I'm missing the eleven o'clock news."

"Oh. Yeah. Sorry, Lieutenant. Well—" He drew a deep, heavy breath. "Well, let's see. First, I got independent confirmation of what Culligan said the bartender told him— that Ricco and this girl came in about three P.M., or so. Her name is Margaret Rath, and she's a B-girl, the way I get it. She worked at the same place Ricco does, down in the Tenderloin."

"Kelley's, you mean."

"Yeah. Right. So, anyhow, they came into the Wayfarer

135

about three, like I said, and they had a couple of drinks, and then they went out in the back. Apparently this happens once or twice a month, according to what I understand. Ricco's already living with someone, like I told you earlier. So, whenever he wants to shack up he uses the Wayfarer. Which is a pretty nice little thing he's got going. Or, rather, *had* going."

"What happened then, Canelli?" I prodded gently.

"Well, the two of them disappeared, like I said. Out in back. That was about three-thirty, by the time they had their drinks, and everything. So then—" He paused for breath. "So then, about fifteen minutes later, the bartender says, this guy came in, and had a drink. And, sure as hell, the guy was Annunzio."

"Did you show the bartender his picture?"

"Yeah. And I turned up a couple of other people, who were in the place between three-thirty and four. And they identified him, too. The only problem is, I didn't have any other pictures, to give them a choice. You know, according to the book. But—"

"Never mind that. What happened next?"

"Well, this guy—Annunzio—he had a drink. He didn't say anything. Didn't do anything. He just had a drink, that's all. So then he put a dollar on the bar, and thanked the bartender, real polite, according to the bartender. And then he went out the back door, like he was going to the can. And that was all."

"What'd you mean, 'that was all'?" I asked irritably.

"I mean that about fifteen minutes or so later the bartender apparently figured out that Annunzio wasn't coming back. Or maybe it was a half hour later. He got busy, he says, and he isn't sure. So, anyhow, he went to the men's room, and checked. It was empty. So he opened the fire door and saw that the outside service door to the sidewalk was unbolted. So he figured that the guy went out that way—which happens sometimes, he says. Especially if the

136

fire door isn't barred. Which it wasn't, because of Ricco and his girlfriend, Margaret."

"Didn't the bartender hear anything? Any shots?"

"No," Canelli answered. "Nobody else did either, that I could find. And I bet I know why they didn't."

I decided not to ask him why.

"I guess it won't be official, until the M.E. digs out the bullets," Canelli continued, "but the holes in the victims' foreheads look like .22 holes. Which makes sense, if Annunzio was the one. I mean, you keep hearing about how those Mafia hit men are using high-speed .22 hollow points because they can be silenced, and there's no ballistic markings when the bullets self-destruct. So I figured that—"

My front-door buzzer sounded. "What's that?" Canelli asked.

"Someone's at the door."

"At this time of night?"

"Apparently," I answered. "Is there anything else, Canelli?"

"Not really, Lieutenant. I'm still trying to find someone who saw Annunzio leave by way of the sidewalk door. But so far, no luck."

The buzzer sounded again—a longer, more decisive buzzing. "I'd better answer the door. I'll see you at the Hall tomorrow morning. You don't mind coming in on Saturday, do you?"

"I don't mind, Lieutenant," he answered cheerfully.

"Good. Thanks. Goodnight, Canelli."

"Good night, Lieutenant. And thank you. For putting me in charge, and everything. I mean, what I said before—about being bugged by the reporters, and everything—I didn't mean that to sound like—"

For the third time the buzzer sounded—angrier, longer.

"Goodnight, Canelli."

I hung up the phone, gathered my bathrobe around me and walked barefooted down the hallway to my front door.

I switched on the outside light and put my eye to the peep-hole. I saw a stranger's face: a middle-aged, well-groomed man wearing a white shirt, an old school tie, an expensive-looking gabardine topcoat and an establishment felt hat. His face, too, was establishment: thin and ascetic-looking, with a long, pinched nose, a severe mouth and disapproving eyes behind noncommittal tortoise-shell glasses. He wore a small, neatly trimmed gray mustache.

As I watched, the stranger moved aside to reveal another man: Charles Brautigan, the FBI's local agent-in-charge. Reluctantly, I opened the door. I'd never liked Brautigan, and he'd never liked me—or any municipal cop, I suspected.

"Hello, Lieutenant." Brautigan offered an indifferent hand. "Sorry to bother you at this hour, but something's come up. Something important." He gestured to the man beside him. "This is Calvin Forbes. He's out from Headquarters, in D.C. We've just come from the airport, in fact." Brautigan's thin, reedy voice was clipped, pitched to a brisk, impersonal note. He'd gone to Yale, and affected an Ivy League accent. He was a tall, improbably handsome man with clear blue eyes and thick, theatrically waved gray hair. Presumably to reinforce his Ivy League image, Brautigan never wore anything but tweed suits, button-down shirts and old school ties. His shoes, he'd once revealed, were custom-made.

When Forbes didn't offer his hand, I turned and led the way into my living room. I normally kept the room picked up. Tonight, though, I'd been going through newspapers I hadn't read for three days. The room was hopelessly littered with papers, an empty cup and glass, and the remnants of a dinner I'd eaten in front of the TV. I switched off the TV, scooped newspapers from the sofa and gestured them to sit down. As I sat in my easy chair, I saw Brautigan staring at my bare feet. Suddenly my feet felt cold.

"This won't take long," Brautigan said. "At least, I hope

it won't take long. We wanted to catch you now, instead of talking to you tomorrow, at the Hall. For reasons that'll be obvious."

Forbes had been trying unsuccessfully to fit his impeccably creased felt hat on the small lamp table beside him. Now he moved the lamp precariously close to the edge of the table, settled his hat to his satisfaction and turned to face me.

"It's about the Murdock murder," Forbes said. Predictably, his voice was dry and precise, subtly condescending. His gaze was fixed on a point that seemed to lie just above my left shoulder. "As soon as I got the details, I decided to come out immediately."

"Calvin is a deputy director of the Bureau," Brautigan intoned. As he spoke I saw Forbes's mouth tighten under the precisely trimmed mustache. Disapproval flickered in his eyes. I wondered whether Brautigan had ever before called Forbes by his first name—or whether he would ever do it again.

"I understand," Forbes said, "that you and Barbara Murdock found Eliot Murdock's notes. I also understand that the notes were, ah, substantive."

"Would you excuse me for just a minute?" I rose and walked down the hallway to my bedroom. My slippers were beside the bureau. Xeroxed copies of Murdock's notes and the affidavits were inside the bureau, under my shirts. I put on the slippers and returned to the living room, explaining, "My feet were cold. Sorry."

Both men projected lofty tolerance as Forbes allowed a calculated moment of silence to pass before he said, "The notes, we understand, are substantive, as I said. So, just as soon as possible, we'd like to have copies of them. The affidavits, too. Especially, the affidavits."

"Are you investigating Murdock's murder?"

"No. Not directly. But, tangentially, we're investigating

it—as part of another investigation we've been conducting."

"Does your investigation concern the Pentagon?"

Forbes and Brautigan exchanged a quick, inscrutable look before Forbes said quietly, "You have seen them, then. The notes and the affidavits. You admit you found them."

Aware that I was suddenly enjoying an unaccustomed sensation of superiority, I slowly, deliberately nodded. "Yes, we found them. They were in the safe at the Beresford Hotel. Now they're at the Hall, in the evidence room."

"Did you read them?"

I nodded. "Yes," I answered cautiously. "Yes, I read them."

"And?"

"And it's pretty heavy stuff," I answered. "It's so heavy, in fact, that I don't have the authority to turn over copies to you. Not without getting clearance."

Behind the tortoise-shell glasses, Forbes's eyes hardened. "I don't think you understand, Lieutenant—" Edging the "Lieutenant" with calm malice, he managed to express all the smooth, subtle contempt that FBI agents could level against men who began their careers in uniform, wearing a gun and a badge. "We're working different sides of the street, you and I. You're concerned with Murdock's murder. I'm not concerned with Murdock. At least, not directly. I'm concerned with—other things."

Again, the patronizing accent on the last two words clearly suggested the disdain Forbes felt.

Even though I knew it was a mistake, I couldn't resist saying, "You mean that you're concerned with Baxter Wardell."

Forbes looked at me for one long, spiteful moment before he picked up his hat and rose to his feet. He didn't move the lamp back to the center of the end table.

"I didn't come three thousand miles to fence with you, Lieutenant."

I decided not to reply. Still seated, uncomfortable in my bathrobe and bare legs, I suddenly felt like a schoolboy being disciplined by the principal. But I knew that I would feel even more inadequate, scrambling to my feet to face him.

"Mr. Brautigan said you'd understand why it's desirable for us to keep this—uncomplicated. I hope, for all our sakes, that he's right." Forbes let a beat pass before he continued. "You say you need 'clearance.' I doubt it—but I'm not inclined to press the point. Besides, I need sleep. So we'll defer this until tomorrow morning. Mr. Brautigan will call you at ten o'clock, to find out whether you've gotten your clearance. Then we'll—" Another bullying beat passed before he said, "We'll decide on appropriate action."

Without looking back, he walked down the hallway to the front door. "Get the goddamn clearance, Hastings," Brautigan muttered. "Get it, or it's your ass."

At the door, Forbes had stopped to put on his hat, carefully settling it on his beautifully barbered head. Forsaking dignity, Brautigan loped to the front door, opened it and gestured for Forbes to precede him.

Sixteen

Placidly puffing his cigar, Friedman glanced at the clock. The time was nine-thirty. On a Saturday morning only Friedman, Canelli, Culligan and myself were manning the Homicide detail. Out in the squad room Culligan was catching the incoming calls. Canelli had gone to the coroner's office, waiting for the Ricco autopsy to furnish us with the bullets that had killed Ricco. In my office Friedman and I looked at each other across a desk strewn with Xeroxed copies of Murdock's notes.

"Actually," Friedman said, gesturing to the copies, "there isn't a whole hell of a lot of substance there. As I read them, the affidavits are all pretty vague. And the notes aren't much more than shorthand."

"I thought the affidavits would be more explicit. It seems as though everyone's trying to screw the other guy without getting screwed himself."

"Exactly. Only the one guy—Simpson, whoever he is— seems to have a handle on anything he's willing to talk about. And, for all we know, Simpson could be the janitor."

"Janitors empty wastebaskets, you know."

Shrugging, Friedman blew a long, lazy plume of smoke toward the ceiling. "I wonder if Calvin Forbes is after Wardell," he mused. He aimed his cigar at the affidavits. "There's no mention of Wardell in those. And sure as hell, Murdock's notes won't constitute evidence. Especially against a big fish like Wardell."

"If Wardell's involved, he's working through intermediaries."

Friedman nodded. "Several intermediaries, probably." He considered a moment, then said thoughtfully, "I wonder whether Wardell's in favor with the current administration in Washington."

"What difference does it make?"

"If he's fallen out of favor, they might be trying to nail him for past transgressions. It happens."

"Maybe Barbara Murdock would know."

"Maybe."

Now I looked at the clock. In twenty minutes Brautigan would call. "I still think," I said, "that we'll be taking a big chance, turning those copies over to the FBI without getting clearance from Dwyer. Especially after the Blake and Ricco murders. This is the time to cooperate with Dwyer, not play games with him."

Friedman raised a pudgy, placating palm. "We aren't going to just turn them over. We're going to do a little horse-trading.We're going to show a profit on the transaction."

"*You're* going to do a little horse-trading. I'm going to hold your coat."

"Trust me," he said. "No one diddles the FBI better than I diddle the FBI."

"Or enjoys it more," I answered.

"Or enjoys it more. Right. I—"

My phone rang.

"Remember," said Friedman, sotto voce, "if it's Forbes or Brautigan, get a meeting on neutral ground. The FBI

loves that cloak-and-dagger stuff. The spookier the better."
As he spoke he lifted a "listen only" extension phone.

I lifted my own phone to hear: "It's Canelli, Lieutenant."

"Oh."

"Expecting someone else, huh? Want me to hang up?"

"It's all right. What've you got?"

"I'm over at the coroner's. And, sure enough, the bullets in Ricco were .22 hollow points, just like I figured. Which is a bummer because there's no ballistics. But the good news is the lab lifted a sharp, clear print from the door of the men's room at the Wayfarer. Maybe Annunzio went in there to put on gloves, before he did the job. Because that's whose print it was. Annunzio's."

"Great. Now all we have to do is find Annunzio."

"Yeah," he answered ruefully. "Right." Then: "Is there anything else, Lieutenant?"

"Not really—except to keep looking for Annunzio."

"What about Walter Frazer? Want me to spend a little time on him?" I looked questioningly at Friedman, still holding the receiver to his ear. He shrugged, then nodded.

"Give it a try," I answered. "But keep in touch with Culligan. Lieutenant Friedman and I are going out in a few minutes."

"Yes, sir. Wish me luck."

To myself, I smiled. Aside from looking and acting like anything but a detective, Canelli's greatest professional asset was an incredibly long-running streak of innocent good luck. With every policeman in San Francisco searching for a mass murderer, Canelli would answer his doorbell to find the killer on his doorstep, asking directions to his next victim's house.

"Good luck, Canelli," I said, breaking the connection.

"What would our lives be without Canelli?" Friedman said. "What would we do for our chuckle a day?" When I didn't reply he said, "Incidentally, did you see the *Sentinel* this morning?"

144

"No."

"Your friend Barbara Murdock has been giving press conferences."

"Press conferences?"

"Right. As I predicted day before yesterday, the newshounds are closing ranks around their fallen comrade, airbrushing in a determined jaw and fearless eyes and a cape flung over his shoulders, and like that. And Barbara, apparently, is using the opportunity to put the heat on."

"How do you mean, 'put the heat on'?"

"She's saying that her father was onto something very big and very wicked in Washington—that he was getting so close to some very important people that he was shut up."

"All of which may be true."

"Granted. But the part I didn't much like was the part about how she implies that those same VIPs are seeing to it that Murdock's murderer goes unpunished."

"Does she mention Wardell by name?"

"Of course not. She doesn't even imply that she's talking about Wardell. Tactically, that's smart. She implies that she knows a lot more than she's telling. Which she does, in fact. But, still, she shouldn't be doing it. Because she's making us look bad. She's making us look like we're taking a dive, because of political pressure. Which, of course, happens to be the truth, at least as far as Dwyer is concerned. Except that we're getting tarred with the same brush. You and me."

"She could also be getting herself in a lot of trouble," I mused. "A *lot* of trouble. If Annunzio thinks she knows more than she really knows—" I let the ominous thought go unfinished.

"Exactly." Friedman dropped his burnt-out cigar stub into my ashtray. "If I were you," he said, "I'd tell her that—"

My phone rang. I waited for Friedman to pick up the extension, then answered. The time was exactly ten o'clock.

"It's Charles Brautigan, Lieutenant."

"Oh—yes." I tried to sound casual, as if I'd just remembered that he was going to call.

"Have you got your clearance?"

"Well—yes and no."

"What's *that* supposed to mean?" he snapped.

"It's supposed to mean that Lieutenant Friedman and I have decided to try and help you. But we're doing it on our own authority. So it's got to be off the record. We've got to be careful."

"The more careful the better," he answered. Then, peevishly, "Mr. Forbes made that plain last night, I thought."

"Mr. Forbes." Not "Calvin." I tried to imagine the scene that precipitated the change.

"Well," Brautigan was saying, "how'll we handle it?"

"Where are you?"

"At the Federal Building."

"Why don't you walk down to Market Street and Larkin and stand in the bus stop on the northwest corner? We'll pick you up in twenty minutes. We'll be driving a green Plymouth Horizon."

He repeated the instructions and abruptly broke the connection.

"There they are—" Friedman pointed.

I swung the Plymouth to the curb behind a bus—and promptly heard another bus horn abusing us from behind. Friedman swung the rear door open. Brautigan gestured Forbes inside, then folded his long, elegantly dressed frame into the cramped rear seat. Friedman, I noticed, had pushed his seat back as far as possible.

"This is Mr. Forbes," Brautigan said, gracelessly introducing Friedman. "Mr. Calvin Forbes, from Washington. Mr. Forbes is a deputy director of the Bureau."

Half turned in his seat, Friedman said, "Hello, Calvin. My name is Pete."

I tried to see Forbes's expression in the mirror but couldn't. Leaning the other way, I looked at Brautigan. He could have been sucking a lemon.

"I thought we'd drive down to the Marina Green," I said. "In a half hour, the *Enterprise* is coming in through the Golden Gate."

"The *Enterprise?*"

"It's an aircraft carrier."

"Yes," Brautigan said stiffly. "We know."

On a cold, gray Saturday morning in November, with rain threatening, the Marina Green was populated almost entirely by hard-core joggers and weekend athletes doggedly circling the ten-acre expanse of grass that bordered the bay. In the center of the green an amiable girls-and-boys touch-football game was beginning. Ignoring the prohibiting sign, renegade dog owners looked the other way while their pets relieved themselves on one of the city's premier playing fields.

"I'd like to bust them," Friedman muttered, staring balefully at the offenders. "I swear to God, if I had a citation book, I'd bust them. Every one of them."

I pulled into a parking place that faced the bay. In another fifteen minutes, despite the threatening weather, all the parking places would be filled, anticipating the *Enterprise*'s arrival. As I switched off the engine and turned in my seat, Forbes spoke for the first time. "Have you got the documents?"

"Yes," Friedman answered. "We've got them." He turned in his seat, facing Forbes.

"Are they originals or copies?"

"Copies."

"Good." Forbes snapped open a black-and-chrome attaché case and placed it on the seat beside him.

"We should warn you, though," Friedman said, "that they aren't as sensational as you might expect from reading

147

today's newspapers." He made no move to hand over the big manila envelope he'd placed on the floor at his feet. I wondered whether Brautigan and Forbes had seen the envelope when they'd gotten into the car. I didn't think so.

"Are they complete?" Forbes asked. "Are you turning over everything you've got?"

"They're complete. But they're—" Friedman hesitated. This, I knew, was the beginning of the game—the sting. "But they're—puzzling. And we, ah, were hoping that you could fill us in."

"Lieutenant Friedman—" Like an exasperated, long-suffering schoolteacher deciding how best to deal with a wayward pupil, Forbes paused. Then, "I'm afraid I don't have time for this. It's eleven o'clock. Even if I'm lucky enough to catch a one o'clock flight, I still won't be home before ten tonight. So you'll—"

"When did you get into San Francisco?" Friedman asked. His face was blandly inscrutable. His voice was polite. Deceptively polite, I knew.

"Last night," Forbes answered shortly. "And—"

"Did you come all the way out here just for the notes?" Friedman inquired innocently. "Six thousand miles, round trip?"

Eyes snapping dangerously, Forbes didn't reply. Instead, he glanced sharply at Brautigan, as if to ask how he'd come to be sitting in a strange car, in an unfamiliar city, being interrogated by an inferior. Finally, speaking in a tightly controlled voice, he said, "Those notes might have a bearing on a current investigation the Bureau is conducting, Lieutenant. Therefore, we appreciate the trouble you've gone to, getting them to us. And we appreciate your, ah, discretion. On this one we'd just as soon not go through channels. However, as I've said, my time is limited. So if you don't mind—" Impatiently fingering the attaché case's lock, he let it go unfinished. Once more he threw a sharp, impatient glance at Brautigan.

"We don't mean to hold you up," Friedman answered equably. "And I'm glad you appreciate the trouble we've taken. But I'm afraid I didn't make myself clear—" For emphasis, he paused. Forbes turned in his seat to stare out toward the Golden Gate, registering haughty disinterest in Friedman. But as the silence lengthened oppressively, he was finally forced to return his gaze to Friedman. With that accomplished, Friedman continued smoothly. "What I'm suggesting," he said, "is an exchange of information."

Forbes's small, humorless mouth twisted into something that could have been an ironic smile. "I see."

In reply, Friedman inclined his head in a mockingly urbane nod—only partly concealing his cat-and-mouse grin.

"I'm afraid I don't have the authority to pass along information on a current case," Forbes answered.

"Well, strictly speaking, neither do we. But we're willing to make an—"

"You have all the authority you need, Friedman," Brautigan snapped. "So, if you don't mind, let's cut the crap. Cal—Mr. Forbes is a busy man. He hasn't come all the way out from Washington to sit here and play games. He—"

"We're not playing games," I interrupted sharply. "We're looking for information. So are you. We can help each other. What's the problem?"

"The problem," Forbes said icily, "is that I'm heading an investigation that could reach high up. Very, very high up. And I simply can't compromise that investigation."

"Well, we're investigating a murder," I retorted. "To you that might not seem like a very big deal. But—"

"What Frank's saying," Friedman said softly, "is that we take our jobs just as seriously as you do—Calvin."

I saw Forbes's expression turn murderous—then saw his eyes drawn inexorably past Friedman, out to the Golden Gate. Turning, I saw the huge, squared-off prow of the *Enterprise* moving slowly beneath the bridge. On the sun-less, sullen day, with the clouds lying dark and heavy on the horizon, the enormous gray shape of the aircraft carrier was materializing in the heavy haze like some silent, ghostly shade—implacable and immense, yet somehow without substance, come from another world. Above its bow and stern, two helicopters hovered like huge, predatory insects. On its flight deck, precisely aligned, rows of supersonic fighters squatted with wings folded, canopies gleaming, vertical fins ranked like broadswords. Dozens of pleasure boats had fallen in beside the monstrous gray shape. Moving beside the carrier through the haze, the pleasure boats lost color and definition, as if their essence had been mysteriously sapped by the warship. Only a fire-boat, spewing a bouquet of white plumes high in the air, lightened the scene.

For a long moment, reluctantly, the four of us shared a moment of awed silence. Then I heard Forbes say, "What is it, exactly, that you think you need? What kind of information?"

I saw the corner of Friedman's mouth twitch as he suppressed a smug little smile. He'd won. In his private war against the establishment, he'd won another skirmish.

Winning, he was always generous. Turning to face Forbes, he spoke somberly and concisely. "We think," he said, "that Murdock was murdered because of something he discovered in Washington, or something that somebody was afraid he might discover. We suspect that the Mafia might have been involved."

"Why do you say that?" Brautigan asked suspiciously.

"Because the killer was probably Joey Annunzio."

Forbes's eyes sharpened. "Out of Miami?"

Watching Forbes warily, Friedman nodded. I knew what he was thinking. If Annunzio crossed state lines to commit murder, or to escape prosecution, the FBI could claim jurisdiction.

"Annunzio—" Forbes looked away, absently watching the slow, inexorable progress of the *Enterprise*.

"We also suspect," Friedman said, "that Baxter Wardell could be involved in a scheme to defraud the Pentagon— the scheme that Murdock was investigating. We think that Murdock came to San Francisco to check out Baxter Wardell. Therefore, we think it's possible that Murdock was killed to prevent him from exposing Wardell. Which is to say—" For emphasis, he let a beat pass. "Which is to say," he repeated, "that, logically, Wardell could have hired Annunzio to kill Murdock. Which gets us to Wednesday night, when Murdock was killed."

Forbes was shaking his head. But it was a thoughtful gesture, not one of denial, or disagreement. "I don't see Baxter Wardell hiring a hood. That's like saying the President would go with a streetwalker. It just wouldn't happen."

"Which isn't to say that Presidents haven't been known to play around, though," I said.

"Where's Annunzio now?" Brautigan asked.

"We think he's still in San Francisco," Friedman replied. "We think he's killed two men here, just yesterday—accomplices in the Murdock murder. Low-level, expendable accomplices."

"Why did he kill them?" Forbes asked.

"To shut them up, probably. His driver, a local hood named Richard Blake, was arrested Wednesday night at the scene. Annunzio was probably afraid he'd talk. And he was right to be afraid. The driver did talk. Unfortunately, he didn't know much."

"How did Annunzio kill him, if he was taken at the scene?" Brautigan asked.

"He was released yesterday," Friedman answered briefly. "We made a deal, so we didn't charge him. We had to release him."

"It couldn't be that you put him out for bait, could it?" Brautigan asked.

Silently, Friedman and I exchanged a look.

"Who's the other victim?" Forbes asked.

"A Tenderloin-type named Ricco. A bartender. He was probably Annunzio's local contact."

"That's a pattern," Forbes said, still following the *Enterprise* with his eyes. "It's where these big-shot hit men are vulnerable. They've got to contact people on the local scene, to set things up for them—fill them in."

Another moment of silence passed, this time thoughtfully—without tension. Somehow the slow, inexorable passage of the *Enterprise* had put our differences into perspective. Finally clearing the Golden Gate Bridge, the giant warship, seen so close, obscured much of the Marin hills across the bay from the Marina Green. It was as if some of the world had ended at the carrier.

"That's really all we've got," Friedman said, a note of finality in his voice. "The rest is speculation."

"Have you actually talked to Baxter Wardell?" Brautigan asked.

"Once," Friedman said. "Briefly."

"And inconclusively," I added.

"Did you question him about—" Forbes hesitated. "About any irregularities concerning Pentagon procurement?"

"Not really," Friedman answered. "We—hinted at it, to get a reaction."

"And what kind of reaction did you get?"

"He tried to blow us off the track," Friedman answered. "He gave us a blast, and then left. Quick."

"What about you?" I asked Forbes. "Have you interrogated Wardell?"

"No," he answered slowly. "No, I haven't. Not yet. It's, ah, not that easy, getting through to him. At least, not in Washington." He looked at me thoughtfully before he said, "I'm surprised you were able to do it."

152

"We caught him by surprise."

Forbes shook his head. "I doubt it."

"Maybe he wanted to find out how much we knew," Friedman mused.

"I assume that the FBI has intelligence on Wardell," I said, looking squarely at Forbes. "I assume you've got a *lot* of intelligence." I saw him nod. Then, plainly reluctant, he began talking. Speaking in a dry, precise voice, as if he were reading from a transcript, he said, "Approximately two years ago, a man named George Simpson got into difficulties with his superiors. Simpson was an efficiency expert at the Pentagon. He's a—" Forbes hesitated, searching for the right word. "He's an unpleasant—an egotistical man. But he's a bright man, too—a genius, some say. When his recommendations for streamlining procurement procedures were ignored, he went over his bosses' heads—unsuccessfully. After that, his job became harder. His superiors, you see, were trying to force him to resign. And about that time his wife left him. By some accounts he slipped his tether a little—didn't give a damn what happened to him. Anyhow, the result was that Simpson decided to go public. He talked to reporters about some rather dramatic cost overruns. At first, he didn't talk about anything illegal. Just inefficiency, and wastefulness, and stupidity. As a result, he found himself down in the documents section, working as a file clerk. He hadn't been demoted in grade, so he didn't have an actionable case. He was just reassigned—or so he was told.

"Matters stayed like that for about six months, during which time it seems that Simpson actually became a little—" Again, Forbes paused, slightly frowning as he searched for the word—"a little paranoid, I'd say. Whether it was his failure on the job or the failure of his marriage isn't clear. It was probably a combination. In any case, at about that time he decided to contact Eliot Murdock, with whom Simpson had had some dealings in the past. He also contacted the Bureau. I gather that he gave Murdock the same information he gave us. It was entirely hearsay, of course. But it was high-voltage stuff. He said that an undersecretary of defense had entered into a kickback scheme with a so-called international arms cartel."

"How did the scheme work?" Friedman asked.

"It worked very simply," Forbes answered dryly. "The undersecretary simply declared certain armaments surplus, and put their price floor way below the market. There was an auction—a rigged auction. The buyer was a company called International Procurement Incorporated—I.P.I., for short. I.P.I. began selling the arms all over the world, for an estimated net profit of thirty million dollars, at least. Meanwhile, the undersecretary resigned—and opened a Swiss bank account. So far, we've traced carefully laundered deposits to that account totaling more than two million dollars."

"And Baxter Wardell owns I.P.I.," I said.

"Not wholly," Forbes said, "but substantially. He followed a formula that's common in matters like this. In exchange for 'services rendered,' so called, he gave away small blocks of stock in I.P.I. to a few extremely well-placed, prestigious people. That way, if there's an investigation, they'll get hurt, too. So, effectively, they act as a shield." Forbes shook his head. "It's incredible how often we see that pattern. Perfectly innocent, unsuspecting people lend their names to all kinds of marginal schemes."

"They profited, though," Friedman suggested. "They were a little too greedy, maybe."

Reluctantly, Forbes nodded. "It's the so-called 'little bit of larceny in all of us,' I suppose. Without which the pigeon-drop con, for example, could never work. Anyhow, that's where we are now. We've been working on the case for months, tracing that laundered money. And after all that time and effort it's still doubtful whether Justice will indict. Which is the reason I'm here. We know about those affidavits Murdock had taken. We want to look at them."

154

"I'm afraid," Friedman said, "that you'll be disappointed." He reached down for the manila envelope and passed it back to Forbes. "To me, most of it looks like pretty soft stuff."

As Forbes unfastened the clasp and impatiently riffled through the contents, I looked again at the *Enterprise.* Bound for the Oakland Naval Base, the carrier was entering the narrows between Alcatraz and Fisherman's Wharf, where less than two hundred yards separated the ship from the shore. With plumes of black smoke streaming from their stacks, gray Navy tugs were nudging at the carrier's sides, curving high above them. In their dress blues, sailors lined the carrier's fantail, waving at the escorting pleasure boats. On one of the sailboats I could make out a colorfully dressed group of girls, all waving wildly. As I watched, a sailor took off his white cap and sailed it toward the small boat.

Seventeen

Seated behind a small walnut writing desk, the City Club's receptionist looked down at my badge, looked me up and down once, then looked a last time at the badge, resigned. He couldn't have been more than thirty years old, but his pale eyes were curiously empty, as if they were incapable of registering pleasure, or pain, or passion. His long patrician nose was fastidiously pinched; his mouth was primly pursed as he asked, "What can I do for you, Lieutenant?"

"We'd like to see Mr. Wardell."

"Concerning what, please?"

"Concerning the matter we discussed with him yesterday," Friedman said.

"Which was?"

"Which was police business."

Sighing, the young man lifted his telephone, touched a button on an illuminated console and waited. Finally: "I'm afraid Mr. Wardell isn't in." Obviously relieved, he replaced the telephone and turned his attention to a magazine.

"When is Mr. Wardell expected back?" I asked.

Sighing again, he slid out a small drawer, opened a morocco-bound notebook and riffled a few pages. "Mr. Wardell didn't leave word," he said stiffly. "Sorry."

Leaning forward, Friedman placed both of his hands flat on the tooled-leather desk top. On the small desk his hands looked very large. Startled, the young man looked up, frowning peevishly.

"It is important that we talk to Mr. Wardell," Friedman said softly. "It is very, very important. Therefore, we're perfectly prepared to go as high up in your organization as is necessary to locate Mr Wardell, or to find out when he's coming back."

As Friedman was speaking, the young man's attention was drawn irresistibly in the direction of the lobby door. I saw him blink, then saw his face fall. Friedman and I turned in unison to face Baxter Wardell striding briskly toward us. Today he wore a cashmere sports jacket and contrasting brown slacks. His white shirt was open at the throat. He was flanked on either side by conservatively dressed men with graying hair and serious eyes. Both of the men carried attaché cases. Each man walked a discreet step behind Wardell.

Friedman stepped forward, offering his hand—which Wardell ignored. "Sorry to trouble you again, Mr. Wardell," Friedman said amiably. "But I wonder if we could have another few minutes of your time?" As he spoke, I moved to stand beside him. Together, we blocked passage down the corridor that led to the elevators and the club's interior. Friedman glanced pointedly toward the door of the visitors' room, off the central hallway to the left. Wardell came to a stop a bare two feet from Friedman's sizable chest.

"Not now, Lieutenant," he said coldly. "I've got a conference scheduled upstairs. I'm leaving immediately afterward for Los Angeles."

"This won't take long," Friedman said quietly. "And it's important. Very important."

157

"I'm sorry, but—"

"It concerns the FBI," I said. "We've just come from a meeting with them. We thought we should talk to you as soon as possible."

"The—" Momentarily, Wardell hesitated. "The FBI?" Covertly, he glanced aside, toward one of the two men beside him. Finally he turned sharply to the door of the visitors' room, throwing an order over his shoulder: "I'll be upstairs in ten minutes. Start without me. Put the environmental-impact projections first on the agenda."

With identical expressions, the two men studied us for a long, inscrutable moment before they walked silently down the hallway to the elevators. Wardell, meanwhile, had already disappeared inside the visitors' room.

Friedman nudged me in the ribs, winked, followed Wardell through the tall oak door. Wardell had gone to the long refectory table, where he turned and confronted us with arms folded, leaning gracefully against the table. Impeccably dressed in the cashmere jacket, utterly at ease in the elegantly paneled room, Wardell could have been posing for a *Town & Country* photographer. Like all consummate actors, Wardell's persona changed with the role he played. Yesterday, dressed in his bush jacket and Wellington boots, he'd personified the wealthy sportsman: dashing, charming, a little reckless. Today, he was the casual man of the world: urbane, haughty, completely in control.

"Well," he asked quietly, "what is it?"

Closing the door behind him, Friedman faced Wardell for a moment, setting the tone with a long, somber stare. Then, politely, he asked whether Wardell had enjoyed flying the newly acquired B-25.

"The aileron boosters malfunctioned," Wardell said shortly. "So I didn't fly."

"Well," Friedman said easily, "you've still got the P-51."

"In which I'm leaving for Los Angeles Burbank very shortly," Wardell snapped. "So let's get on with it, please. What's this about the FBI?"

"Yesterday," Friedman said, "we questioned you about a surplus-arms scandal that Eliot Murdock was investigating. Last night, a deputy director of the FBI arrived from Washington. It turns out that the FBI has been investigating the same scandal for months. We don't know all the details of the story, but it apparently concerns an undersecretary of defense and Swiss bank accounts and kickbacks—and a man named Simpson, who blew the whistle."

During Friedman's brief monologue, I watched Wardell's face, searching for some telltale reaction. I was disappointed. As Friedman talked, Wardell simply stared—first at Friedman, then at me. His face revealed absolutely nothing. His gray eyes were cold, utterly emotionless. When Friedman had finished, Wardell allowed a long, deliberate moment of silence to pass before he said softly, "And where, exactly, do I fit into all this?"

"The firm that's under investigation is I.P.I.," I said.

"We understand that you're connected with I.P.I." Friedman spoke softly, gently.

"And," I continued, "since both Murdock and the FBI were investigating I.P.I.—and since Murdock could have been killed for his trouble—we've got some questions we'd like to ask you."

"We've already covered that yesterday," Wardell said icily. "I never met the man. Except by reputation, I never knew him."

"What about a man named Joey Annunzio?" Friedman asked. "Did you ever meet him?"

"Joey Annunzio?" He was frowning, puzzled. "Who's Joey Annunzio?"

"What about a bartender named Ricco?" I pressed. "Have you ever heard of him?"

"No."

"How about Walter Frazer?" Friedman asked, picking up the harsh tempo. "Is he known to you?"

Still leaning against the long refectory table, still with his

159

arms folded, apparently relaxed, Wardell looked at each of us in turn. Then, slowly and incredulously, he began to shake his head. "This is unbelievable. Here you are, two underpaid, overworked, not very grammatical city detectives—questioning me like I'm some hoodlum who's under suspicion for purse snatching. You're—Christ—you're even using all the tired old squad-room clichés, trying to whipsaw me, rattle me with your clever, rapid-fire questions. It's—" Still shaking his head, he began to smile: a mirthless twisting of his wide, handsomely sculpted mouth. "It's ludicrous," he said. "Bizarre. Totally bizarre."

Looking him steadily in the eye, Friedman said quietly, "You didn't answer the last question, Mr. Wardell."

Drawing a long, deep breath, Wardell pushed himself deliberately away from the table. "No," he answered, "I haven't. And I don't intend to answer it, either—not that question, or any other question. You've worn out your welcome, Lieutenant. Yesterday, I tried to be patient with you. I tried to help. Then I read the stories that Barbara Murdock gave out about how I was responsible for her father's death because of some illegal Pentagon deal he'd uncovered. And now, for the second day in a row, you're harassing me. Well—" He stepped purposefully toward the door. "Well, it's gone far enough. Whatever ridiculous game you're playing at, it's over. Finished."

I moved between Wardell and the door, at the same time slipping my Miranda card from my shirt pocket. "I think," I said, "that it's time for me to read you your rights, Mr. Wardell. You have the right to—"

"Take that card and shove it, Lieutenant," he blazed, pushing roughly around me. "As for the questions, save them for my lawyers. Because in an hour's time you'll be hearing from my lawyers. You, and Barbara Murdock, and the FBI, too." Leaving the door open, he stalked out of the room.

Standing beside me, Friedman murmured, "He did it again."

160

"Did what again?"

"Talked too much."

"How do you mean?"

"I mean," Friedman said, "that Barbara's barbs, if you'll excuse the expression, seem to have hit the mark. He thinks those stories are all about him. No one else thinks so, as far as I can see. Just him. Just him and us, too." To himself, he nodded, smugly satisfied. "Guilt," he said softly, "it's wonderful. It brings them all down, eventually. The big boys and the little boys, they're all the same. If they're guilty, and you get them talking, they eventually say too much. Every time."

"So what now?" I asked.

"Now," he said, "maybe we should go back to the Hall and see whether we can fit the pieces together."

Eighteen

At the Hall, I found a single sheet of stationery on my desk. *See me immediately* was written across the paper in bold, strong script. The message was signed "J.D." The letterhead was inscribed *James Dwyer, Chief of Police, Hall of Justice, San Francisco, California.*

I'd never before seen the letterhead. Staring at it, I wondered why it didn't include either a street address or a zip code. Speculating, I remembered that the presidential stationery is headed simply, *The White House, Washington, D.C.*

As I was dropping the note in the "in" basket, my phone rang.

"Did you get one, too?" Friedman asked.

"Yes."

"The last time Dwyer was in his office on a Saturday afternoon, there was a mass murderer loose."

I didn't answer.

"Between the two of you," Dwyer said, "you've managed to make a mess of this thing. A total mess. You—Christ—you've antagonized everyone. *Everyone.*"

Seated side by side on Chief Dwyer's long leather sofa, neither Friedman nor I replied. Stealing a glance at Friedman I saw him staring straight ahead. His dark eyes were solemn, his broad, swarthy face revealed nothing. If Friedman ever went to church—or synagogue—I was thinking, this is how he must look.

"What's happened," Dwyer said, "is that we've lost control of this thing. I mean, we have *totally* lost control. And it's getting worse, not better. It's getting worse by the *minute*." Dwyer was pacing back and forth behind his massive walnut desk, gesticulating as he walked. At age sixty, with a full head of dramatic white hair and the square-jawed, broad-browed, florid-faced good looks of a tub-thumping evangelist, Dwyer personified the handsome, successful Irish politician. His complexion glowed with vitality and good health. He was a trim, athletic-looking hundred seventy-five pounds. Accenting his white hair and clear blue eyes, Dwyer always wore gray suits—expensively cut gray suits. His shirts were always a gleaming white; his ties were always a conservative gray silk-on-silk. His cuffs always seemed to protrude exactly an inch from his sleeves, revealing large golden cuff links presented to him by the governor. During his thirty-five years as a San Francisco policeman, Dwyer had never come down on the wrong side of a captain's shuffle or a bloodletting at City Hall. To the media, Dwyer often described himself as a "cop's cop." But the careers of his enemies inside the department were often short—and always unhappy.

"Among other things," Dwyer was saying, "it turns out that we're ass-deep in high-priced lawyers, not to mention prominent people—pissed-off, prominent people. We—" His phone rang. As Dwyer snatched up the receiver and barked that he wasn't to be disturbed, Friedman murmured, "I think they call that alliteration. Pissed-off prominent people. All P's."

Dwyer banged down the phone, braced his hands wide

on the desk and leaned toward us. "That," he said heavily, "was the city attorney calling. Twenty minutes ago CBS news called. And NBC called—and ABC, too. And, frankly, I don't know what to tell them. I mean, I'm hoping—I'm praying—that the two of you, between you, have got some answers that I can give these people. Because I'm telling you—I'm admitting to you—that I'm running out of answers. I mean, I am *really* running out of answers." Still leaning on his wide-braced palms, breathing heavily now, he looked at us each in turn before he said, "Over the years, the two of you have done a good job. We've had our ups and our downs, but I've never denied that you're both good cops. You run a good squad. You've made me look good. That, I appreciate. I've told you about it, too. When everything's going right, I tell you. Which gives me the right to tell you when things *aren't* going right—when you're making me look bad." He drew a long, labored breath. "So I'm telling you," he said solemnly, "that I've never looked worse in my whole thirty-five years on the force than I look right now. And I don't appreciate it. I mean, I *really* don't appreciate the way you're making me look right this minute." Delivered in a voice that trembled with righteous fervor, the speech could have come from a pulpit. Boring into us, Dwyer's blue eyes seemed simultaneously to plead for relief and to warn us of some terrible, unspecified danger.

"You're making me look silly," he said softly, sinking regretfully into his tall leather swivel chair. "Very, very silly."

I heard Friedman clear his throat. Thank God, he was going to start.

"Were, ah, Baxter Wardell's lawyers in touch with you? Is that, ah, the problem?"

Dwyer studied Friedman intently before he said, "The problem isn't that they got in touch with me—which they did, about five minutes after CBS got in touch with me.

The problem is that I didn't *know* they were going to get in touch with me. I didn't even know that Baxter Wardell was in the picture. *That's* the problem." Now Dwyer's voice was ominously low. His mouth was rigid, his eyes fixed. His breathing had deepened, his color had heightened.

"We should have called you," I said—and meant it. "We just now came from interrogating him. We were going to fill you in as soon as we got to the Hall. It never occurred to us that Wardell would get to you so fast."

"Especially on Saturday," Friedman said

"When did the two of you first talk to Wardell?" Dwyer asked.

"That—ah—" Friedman cleared his throat. "That was yesterday, I think. Friday."

"Before or after you and I discussed Jeffrey Sheppard and Avery Rich?"

"That was—ah—before we talked," Friedman admitted.

Dwyer studied Friedman for a long, glowering moment before he said, "What were you trying to do, for Christ's sake? What kind of game were you playing?"

"It wasn't a game," I said. "Until this morning, when we talked to the FBI, we didn't have any real grounds for suspecting Wardell might be involved. So we—"

Dwyer's laser stare turned on me. "Did you say the FBI?" he asked ominously.

As concisely as I could, I outlined the details of Forbes's investigation. As I talked, Dwyer's eyes never left my face. Finally, speaking very quietly, he said, "What's Forbes's title?"

"Deputy director," I admitted. "The—ah—reason he contacted me, he wanted to keep the whole thing at a low level. For, ah, security reasons."

"Because of Wardell," Friedman put in, "and his clout. They don't want to go public until they've really got the goods."

"So you turned over evidence to a deputy director of the

FBI without letting me know." Dwyer rose deliberately from his chair and strode gravely to the far corner of his office, where an American flag rested in its gilded standard. For a moment he stood with his back to us, head bowed, hands clasped behind him. When he finally turned, his expression was solemn.

"I'd like to repeat what I told you before," he said. "You men are good cops. And I like to think that I'm a good cop, too." He paused, waited for us to murmur assent, then began the slow, somber walk to his desk. "And," he said, "whether or not I'm the greatest chief of police in history, I can tell you—both of you—that I plan to be here, in this office, five years from now, when it's retirement time. I already know what I'm going to say at my retirement banquet." He sat down in his leather chair, and absently caressed the gleaming top of his walnut desk. As he did, his golden cuff links caught the light from an antique brass desk lamp.

"I'm telling you all this," he said, "so that you'll believe me when I say that this Murdock thing has made me look worse than I've ever looked in my whole thirty-five years on the force. And I'm also telling you that I can't afford it. Which is another way of saying that I can't afford what you're doing to me. I can't afford to have two key witnesses killed within a couple of hours of each other. I can't afford to have the media discover that we were looking for Ricco—and couldn't find him before Annunzio found him. And, furthermore, I can't afford to have them find out that we already had Blake in custody, for God's sake, and then released him. And, especially, I can't afford to have you two rousting one of the most important men in the country as if he were a—a Tenderloin pimp." He looked at us both carefully in turn before he asked, "Do you understand what I mean? Do you understand what I'm telling you—what I'm *really* telling you?"

In unison, we nodded. The message was clear. Our jobs were on the line.

"All right," Dwyer said, a note of grim finality in his voice. "We understand each other." Again, he looked at both of us, hard. "Don't we?"

This time, we were required to affirm that, yes, we understood each other.

"All right," he repeated, forcing himself to sit back in his chair. "All right. Now. The first thing I want to know is, are there any more surprises? Anything else I don't know that I should know?"

"No, sir," Friedman answered. As he spoke I glanced at him. I couldn't remember him ever calling Dwyer "sir."

"As I understand it," Dwyer said, "all we've really got left—the only possibility—is that we'll turn up Annunzio. Is that about it?"

"That's about it," I admitted.

"And Baxter Wardell—" Dwyer winced, as if the name caused him pain. "There's no hard evidence connecting Wardell with Murdock's murder. Is that right?"

I looked at Friedman who said, "Except for Murdock's notes, that's right."

"The I.P.I. connection is something else, though," I said. "If the FBI has I.P.I. tied to an arms-fraud scheme at the Pentagon, and if Wardell really controls I.P.I., then there's a connection."

"Forget the goddamn Pentagon," Dwyer snapped. "I'm talking about San Francisco—about Murdock's murder. That's all I care about. And I'm telling you—warning both of you—that I don't want Wardell questioned again about that murder unless it's with my specific approval. Is that clear?"

It was clear, we said.

"We should tell you," Friedman said, "that Wardell plans to leave for Los Angeles this afternoon or evening."

"So?" Dwyer said sarcastically.

"So," Friedman answered gently, "if a connection to the murder should develop, he'll be out of town."

"Is he coming back?"

"We don't know."

"Did you ask him?"

"No. But, if we had asked him, he wouldn't't've answered. He was, ah, pretty uncommunicative, the last we saw of him."

For a moment Dwyer didn't reply. Then: "Let's get back to the notes," he said. "I want you to give copies to Jeffrey Sheppard. Clear?"

Friedman and I exchanged a quick glance. "If you say so," Friedman answered with plain reluctance. "But I don't think that—"

"I want you to *give* them to him," Dwyer said. "They're his property. I want him to have them. I want him and Avery Rich and the mayor off my back. I want Sheppard to get his goddamn notes, and get on a goddamn airplane and get back to New York." For a long, hard moment Dwyer stared at Friedman before he said, "You gave Forbes copies, without my authorization. Now I want you to give Sheppard copies—with my authorization. Is that clear, Lieutenant?"

"Yes, sir," Friedman answered, holding Dwyer's eye. This time the "sir" had been satirically accented.

"And, after you do that," Dwyer continued, "I want you to find Barbara Murdock. I want you to put a muzzle on her. She's making us look silly with all that crap she's handing out."

"Still," Friedman said, "she could be helping. The stuff she's giving out makes it seem like we've got more information than we've actually got. Which could be a plus, if it puts pressure on whoever's giving Annunzio his orders."

"What you're missing, though," Dwyer countered, "is that it's putting pressure on me, which is what this session is all about, in case you've forgotten. It's also putting pressure on Sheppard. It's making him look silly. Which is why, incidentally, he's hired a private detective."

168

"A private detective?" I echoed.

Dwyer nodded. "Sheppard suspected all along that Barbara Murdock had copies of Murdock's notes. So he's had a private detective following her." Dwyer paused, looking at me closely. Then, "Are you sure—absolutely sure—that she doesn't have copies?"

I stared him straight in the eye and let a beat pass before I said, "If she has copies, she didn't get them from me."

"Good," Dwyer said heavily. "At least, that's something. Incidentally, that phone call I took was about Sheppard. He's just arrived here—with his lawyer. I want you to talk to him. I want you to hand copies of Murdock's notes to him, personally. And I want you to apologize. For the Department. Do you understand?" Slowly and reluctantly— still staring squarely at him—I nodded. I'd never liked Dwyer—never admired him. In that moment I could have hit him with my fist. I hoped he could see it all in my face.

He didn't. He suddenly got to his feet, and waited for us to rise. The session was over. After a final warning not to conceal anything more from him, he curtly dismissed us.

Savagely, Friedman punched the "coffee, double-sugar" button and glared at the paper cup as it fell in its holder and began to fill. "For the first time since I made detective," he grated, "I feel like quitting. I feel like going right back down that hallway and knocking on his door and cramming my goddamn badge down his throat. I really do." He snatched the cup from the machine, spilling coffee on the floor.

Watching my own cup fill, I said nothing. I was thinking that Friedman had always called me a "long, slow burner." Until that moment, waiting for my cup of coffee, I'd never realized how right he'd been. It would be a long time before I'd forget the anger I'd felt, listening to Dwyer.

Friedman downed half his coffee in one noisy gulp, then said, "You know what Dwyer's really saying, don't you?"

169

"He's saying that I've got to get down on my knees and kiss Sheppard's ass."

Fervently, he nodded. "I know. It—it's a goddamn obscenity. But that's not the worst of it. What he's really saying—what that was really all about—is that he wants us to lay off Wardell. Dwyer figures that if we connect Wardell to the murder, it could cost him his job. That's what it's all about. Even if Wardell should be convicted, Dwyer would be a casualty. There'd be bodies all over the street. And he knows. He's got a—a rat's instinct for survival."

For a moment I sipped my coffee in silence, grimly imagining my coming confrontation with Jeffrey Sheppard.

"You should've told him about our first talk with Wardell," I said quietly. "That's what started him off. When Wardell's lawyers called, he wasn't prepared."

"Wardell's only part of it," he snapped. "Sheppard and Avery Rich and *Tempo* magazine are the rest of it. He's afraid of them. All of them."

I dropped my empty cup in a trash basket. "I'd better get those copies, and find Sheppard and get it over with. I'll talk to you later."

"Don't kiss his ass," Friedman said earnestly. "Don't *do* it."

"I won't."

Nineteen

I flipped my intercom switch. "All right, send Mr. Sheppard in."

With my jacket buttoned and my tie freshly knotted, I stood behind my desk, waiting. Sheppard knocked once and opened the door without being invited. As he'd done two days before, he entered the office as a general might enter a briefing room, ready to take command. I handed him a bulging manila envelope.

"There's Murdock's notes, Mr. Sheppard. And copies of affidavits, too. Everything that Murdock had with him."

Standing on the other side of my desk, he took the envelope, turned it over once, then dropped it on the desk. He sat down in my visitors' chair, crossed his legs, leaned back in the chair and sat silently for a moment, eyeing me coldly. Finally he said, "How'd you find them?"

"They were in the hotel safe at the Beresford." Reluctantly, I sat down behind the desk. I'd hoped to hand him the copies politely and watch him leave. I should have known better—should have realized he wouldn't forgo his pound of flesh.

He studied me for another long, brutal moment before

he said, "I'm not going to ask when you found them, Lieutenant. I'm going to assume that you found them after we talked, not before."

Hoping he could sense the contempt I felt for his bully-boy bad manners, I didn't reply, didn't allow my eyes to drop.

"Who else besides you has seen these?" he asked, pointing to the envelope.

"Lieutenant Friedman has seen them. And Chief Dwyer. And two men from the FBI."

"Who from the FBI?" he asked intently.

I hesitated, then decided to say, "The local agent in charge has copies—one set of copies. His name is Brautigan. He's shown them to other agents, I imagine. But I'm not sure. You'd have to ask him."

"What about Barbara Murdock? Does she have copies?"

"No, she doesn't." I was aware of the relief I felt, truthfully denying it.

"Has she seen them? Read them?"

I let a beat pass before I said slowly, "Yes, she's seen them. Most of them. The notes, anyhow. And maybe one or two of the affidavits."

"You let her see them? A—a civilian?"

"She helped me find them. We found them together. I felt she was entitled to see them."

"And I feel you exceeded your authority."

"That's your privilege, Mr. Sheppard."

"Chief Dwyer thinks so, too. Very definitely. As you'll discover—if you haven't already."

Instead of responding, I countered with a question. "You've hired private detectives to follow her. Why?"

"You didn't seem to be making much progress finding the notes. I decided to take matters into my own hands. And incidentally, you aren't making much progress shutting her up, Lieutenant."

I suddenly realized that within the space of a few hours,

172

Wardell, Dwyer and now Sheppard had all addressed me by accenting the single word "Lieutenant" with an identical note of casual contempt.

"Is that what your private detectives are doing? Shutting her up?"

Picking up the manila envelope and lightly hefting it, still casually contemptuous, he smiled at me. "It doesn't matter now. I'll take them off the case."

"What agency did you hire?"

"Babcock and Penziner." He turned, strode to the door and stood for a moment with his back to me. Then he turned to face me. For another moment he looked at me with an expression I couldn't read—a thoughtful, speculative expression. Finally, speaking calmly, he said, "You've caused me a lot of trouble, Lieutenant. But, now that I've got what I want, I'll tell you something that you might find instructive—and surprising, perhaps." He waited until he had my full, reluctant attention before he went on. It was, I knew, an inquisitor's trick. I'd used it myself, often. And the trick was working. I wanted to hear what he'd say. So, facing him fully, I gave him the attention he demanded.

"You're the kind of tough, stubborn man that I like and respect," Sheppard said. "Which is more than I can say for your boss. I deal with people like him constantly. They're the kind of people who make the commercial world turn, unfortunately. And the political world, too. But that doesn't mean that I respect them." He pointed to my desk. "I've left my card. When you find out who murdered Eliot Murdock, give me a call. I'll see what I can do about giving you credit." He nodded once, turned and left the office.

I was looking at Sheppard's card, running my thumb lightly across the richly embossed letters, when my phone rang.

"It's Walter Babcock, Lieutenant. Babcock and Penziner. Are you busy? Am I interrupting anything? If you're busy, I can—" He let it go, anxiously unfinished. He spoke quickly and apologetically in a low, colorless voice. Babcock was a small, nervous man with an ulcer, assorted tics and a damp handshake. He could hardly complete a sentence without apologizing for it.

"It's all right." I opened my center desk drawer and dropped Jeffrey Sheppard's card in a small section designed for business cards. "What can I do for you?"

"I'm trying to locate Mr. Sheppard. Jeffrey Sheppard. I understand he's with you."

"He just left, Babcock."

"Oh. Sorry. I'll try his hotel, then. Sorry to have bothered you."

"You've been tailing Barbara Murdock, I understand."

"That's—ah—yes. That's right, Lieutenant. I have. Yes."

"Where is she now? Still at the Beresford?"

"You mean now? Right now? Or do you mean registered?"

"I mean now."

"Right now, as far as I know, she's on her way out of town. She's going up to Marin County. Or, at least, that's where I think she's going. Which is why I'm calling, you see. Or, at least, that's why I'm trying to call Mr. Sheppard. To get travel authorization, I mean. I figured I should—" His voice trailed off into uncertain silence. He was wondering whether he'd said too much—or not enough.

Marin County . . .

"Is she on Wardell's trail?" I asked. "Baxter Wardell? Is that it?"

"That—ah—" Again, his voice faded. "That's—ah—"

"That's it. *Isn't* it?"

"Yeah," he answered uncomfortably. "I mean, I *guess* that's it. I'm not sure, though. Not positive. I—"

My intercom buzzed. "I've got another call, Babcock," I said. "If you find her, I'd like you to call me. If I'm not here, leave a message. Will you do that?"

"I—ah—"

"Do it, Babcock." I switched to the intercom.

"It's Canelli, Lieutenant. Can I see you for a couple of minutes? I just got in from the field, and I think I might have something."

"Come on in, Canelli." I cradled the phone, looked at it for a moment, then dialed Friedman's interoffice number.

"Cooled down yet?" I asked.

"No."

"Anything new?"

"I'm trying to find Annunzio—to take my mind off Dwyer."

"Any luck?"

"No. Any more questions? I've got the Highway Patrol on the other line. A lady tolltaker on the Bay Bridge thinks she saw Annunzio. Which is the fourteenth time, by actual count, that he's been sighted today. Not to mention yesterday. Twenty-seven times. What about you? Anything?"

In a few words I described my conversation with Babcock. As I was speaking, Canelli came in. I gestured him to a chair.

"Babcock is a nebbish," Friedman said. "But he usually has his facts straight."

"I think she's going after Wardell."

"But why?"

"To confront him—shake him up. Who knows?"

"Wardell's on his way to Los Angeles," Friedman said. "In his P-51. Which he keeps in Marin County."

"So?"

"So why don't you call Mrs. Wardell and get the location of Wardell's airstrip? Maybe I'll take a run up there, if it's not too far."

"Dwyer told you—both of us—to stay away from Wardell. We aren't supposed to contact him without Dwyer's permission. What're you doing? Considering a new career?"

"Dwyer also told us to find Barbara," I said. "Remember?"

"I remember," he said sourly. "I'll get back to you. Maybe I'll also call the FAA, and see whether Wardell filed a flight plan." As the line clicked dead, I turned to Canelli. He was sitting on the edge of his chair, looking at me with his soft, anxious eyes. I could see perspiration glistening on his forehead. Whenever Canelli came to my office, he perspired.

"What can I do for you, Canelli? What've you got?" Trying to put him at ease, I leaned back in my chair, smiling.

"Well, ah, I'm not sure, Lieutenant," he said, earnestly frowning—and still perspiring. "But I thought I should tell you about it, anyhow."

"All right—" I spread my hands. "Tell me." As I spoke, my stomach rumbled. I glanced at my watch. The time was almost four-thirty. Except for the cup of coffee I'd had with Friedman, I hadn't eaten anything since breakfast.

"Well," he said, "after I finished my report this morning, I went out and did a little checking on Walter Frazer, like you told me. That was about ten o'clock. Or maybe ten-thirty. I forget. Anyhow, I started with Frazer—but I didn't get anywhere. I mean, he just gave me a lot of double talk about how important he was, and how much he had to do, and everything. So then, I thought I'd do a little checking around the neighborhood, about his car. I mean, I remembered what you said about his car keys. Or key, I mean. One key, when there should've been a whole ringful. So, anyhow, I started checking around. And about the fourth place I went I found this guy named Simcich. He was at home Wednesday night, but he had to leave town Thursday morning, for New York. On business. He's in advertising. Which is why nobody else interviewed him. So, anyhow—" As my stomach continued to rumble, Canelli caught his breath. "So, anyhow, it turns out that on

176

Wednesday night, about eight o'clock, Simcich was upstairs in his bedroom, packing for his trip to New York. Well, he was by his front window, and he happened to look across the street, toward Walter Frazer's place. And he sees someone—a man—come walking down the street and turn in at Frazer's garage. According to Simcich, the guy walks right up to the service door of the garage and goes right inside—which struck Simcich as a little odd. Not *real* odd. But a *little* odd."

"Did he have a key to the service door?"

"Simcich couldn't tell."

"All right. Go ahead."

"Well," Canelli said, "the next thing that Simcich knows, the big garage door comes open, and the guy drives out in Frazer's Buick. Or at least *someone* drives out in the Buick. Simcich couldn't see the guy, inside the car."

"Did Simcich get a good look at him before he went into the garage?"

Regretfully, Canelli shook his head. "Not really, Lieutenant. I mean, he gave a general description of the guy. But it could've fitted a thousand guys—including Annunzio, and Blake, and God knows who else. You know—the old story."

"All right. What happened then?"

"Well, Simcich finished his packing, but he kept thinking about Frazer's car. Apparently they had several thefts in the neighborhood, the way I understand it. So anyhow, after he's packed he decides he'll go across the street and tell Frazer that someone just drove away in his Buick. Which he did. Tell Frazer, I mean."

I realized that I was leaning forward in my chair, intently waiting for what came next.

"And Frazer, according to Simcich, acted pretty strange about the whole thing."

"How do you mean, 'strange'?"

"Well, first of all, he took a long time to come to the

door, Simcich said. And then, when he heard what Simcich had to say, he acted like—" Canelli's brow furrowed. "He acted like he didn't want to be there, or something. I mean, Simcich says that he seemed kind of—" Canelli broke off, searching for the word. "Kind of out of it, sort of. Like he was spaced out, or in shock, or something. That lasted for maybe a minute, Simcich said—until Frazer got a hold on himself, you might say. So then, Simcich says that Frazer said everything was all right—that he knew all along that someone was going to come and get his car, but he'd just forgotten, temporarily. So then, he brushed Simcich off."

"Brushed him off?"

"Yeah. You know—thanked him for his trouble, and closed the door in his face."

"How do you rate Simcich? As a witness?"

Still frowning earnestly—still perspiring—Canelli said, "I rate him pretty high, Lieutenant. I mean, he's obviously a guy with class. He's smart, and he's—you know—he's aware of what's happening."

"Did Simcich say whether or not the garage door was closed after the subject left in the Buick?"

"Jeeze—" Exasperated with himself, Canelli shook his head. "I forgot to ask him. But I can see what you mean. If the guy closed it manually, he probably wasn't a thief. And if it closed automatically, then he must've had an opener."

"And, either way, garage doors make noise when they close."

Somberly, Canelli nodded.

"Did you talk to Walter Frazer after you talked to Simcich?"

"No," he ansered earnestly. "No, I didn't, Lieutenant. I mean, I figured I should talk to you first. You know?"

"I know, Canelli. And you were right." I got to my feet and locked up my desk. "Get the car. I'll meet you out in front."

*   *   *

I braced myself as Canelli swung the cruiser awkwardly into a corner, entering the intersection too fast, and coming out too slowly. With Canelli driving, my cruiser never performed as expected. Canelli was constantly wrestling with the car—and the car fought back. It was all part of Canelli's long, losing battle with the machine. Automobiles were his primary foe, but he was also the helpless victim of coffee machines, tape recorders, typewriter ribbons and walkie-talkie controls. Yet, before he'd wandered into law enforcement, Canelli had been a journeyman electrician. Electricity, he said, made sense.

"What'd we get on Frazer's background check?" I asked. "Did you do it?"

"Culligan did most of it," he answered. "He says that he didn't find out anything very damaging or suspicious. Except that Frazer seems to make a lot of money, considering that he's only thirty-six years old and operates on his own. I mean, he isn't part of a big, high-powered law firm, or anything. He just has a secretary and a research assistant, that's all."

"What kind of law does he practice?"

"Just general stuff. Nothing special. That's what I mean—it's hard to see where his money comes from."

"How much money does he make?"

"His bank says that almost a hundred and fifty thousand dollars went through his commercial account last year."

"For a lawyer and two assistants, that's a lot of money."

"I know. I saw his office. It's nice, but nothing spectacular—just two rooms. The rent is three hundred a month. That's thirty-six hundred a year. Say the phone and stationery and like that costs another three thousand. And say he pays his secretary and his researcher fifteen thousand each, which I doubt. That still leaves—" Canelli frowned, calculating.

"It leaves a lot." I pointed ahead. "The next corner is Jackson. You'd better get in the right lane."

"Oh. Right." Canelli looked hurriedly over his shoulder and swung to the right—too quickly. Behind us, a horn bleated angrily.

"Those goddamn sports cars," he muttered.

We turned into Jackson Street, drove three blocks and parked directly in front of Walter Frazer's building. Across the street, Canelli had stationed a General Works team, on stakeout. I nodded to the two detectives, and raised three fingers as I switched my walkie-talkie to channel three.

"Is he inside?" I asked.

"Yes, sir."

"Does he know you're here?"

"I don't think so."

"All right, we'll take it. You're relieved. Thanks."

"Thank *you*."

Out of long habit, I unbuttoned my jacket and loosened my revolver in its holster as we walked between tall privet hedges to Frazer's front door. The building had been built soon after the turn of the century, originally designed as a rambling, elegant Victorian town house. Its generously curved bay windows overlooked the peaceful, tree-lined street. The building's original gingerbread trim had been meticulously maintained, and was now painted in subtly contrasting colors, accenting the spindles and scrolls and cornices that decorated the three-story façade. On appearance, the overhead garage door was the only concession to contemporary design.

Beside the ornate front door, a thick brass plate was inscribed with the names of three tenants. I pushed the button beside Frazer's name and stepped back from the door, giving myself room. It was another habit I'd learned over the years. Like early aviators who constantly flew with an eye out for an emergency landing spot in case of engine failure, a detective knocking on a strange door has already decided which way he'll jump in case of trouble.

Frazer opened the door the second time I rang the bell.

He was wearing a white terry-cloth robe and slippers. His thinning sandy hair was wet and uncombed, plastered to his skull. In the robe, with his hair in disarray and a day's growth of beard stubbling his face, he no longer resembled the carefully groomed model of the fast-rising executive that I'd seen in my office the morning after Murdock's murder.

"Oh—Lieutenant." Behind his modish gold-framed glasses, Frazer's eyes seemed to contract. He looked at Canelli, frowned, and looked back at me. "What—" He cleared his throat. "What can I do for you?"

"We'd like to talk to you, Mr. Frazer." I moved forward. "May we come in?" I took another purposeful step, forcing him back.

"Well—yes. For a few minutes, anyhow. But I'm going out for dinner, I'm afraid, in less than an hour."

Not replying, I followed him down a short common hallway and into a small, luxuriously furnished ground-floor apartment. The apartment was furnished with antiques, oriental rugs, paintings and floor-to-ceiling shelves that held collections of vases, glassware and statuary. In the living room Frazer went to a brass-studded leather wing chair and immediately sat down without waiting for us to be seated. As we sat side by side on a matching leather sofa, I saw Frazer cross his legs and begin fussily gathering the folds of the terry-cloth robe across his thighs and around his calves. Watching him fidget uncomfortably, I was secretly pleased. In Germany the Nazis often stripped their victims before interrogation, to demoralize them.

Then I remembered my own discomfort when Forbes and Brautigan had surprised me in my bathrobe and bare feet.

"This is Inspector Canelli, Mr. Frazer."

He threw an annoyed glance at Canelli. "Yes. We talked this morning. Briefly."

"Before we start," I said, taking out my Miranda card, "I want to read your rights to you."

"My—my rights? But why?"

Ignoring the question, I repeated the familiar, stilted phrases. When I finished, he stared at me with a puzzled frown. "But I still don't—"

"After Inspector Canelli talked to you, he talked to Mr. Simcich. Your neighbor, across the street."

The V at the neck of Frazer's terry-cloth robe revealed an Adam's apple bobbing convulsively. "Yes," he answered finally, speaking in a low, constricted voice. Then, clearing his throat, he spoke more loudly, more authoritatively: "Yes. Simcich. Wh—" Again, he was forced to clear his throat. "What is it that you want to know?"

"I want to know," I said, "why you told Simcich, on Wednesday night, that your car wasn't stolen—and then told me, on Thursday, that it *was* stolen." With my gaze locked hard into his, I spoke softly, distinctly—ominously. I saw him flinch, saw his eyes flick toward Canelli before they faltered and finally fell. At the same time, the terry-cloth parted to reveal thick fleshy thighs.

"Is—" The tip of his tongue circled his lips. "Is that wh-what Simcich said?"

I nodded. "Yes, Mr. Frazer. That's what he said."

Frazer tried to meet my gaze—and failed. Still licking at his lips, he muttered, "Simcich's back, then. From New York."

I decided not to reply—decided to let a harsh, lengthening silence work for me. Now a muscle high on Frazer's cheek began to twitch. At his temple a vein was throbbing. Behind the gold-framed glasses, his eyes were circling the richly furnished room, involuntarily seeking escape.

"Maybe Annunzio should have killed Simcich, too," Canelli said. "Like he did Blake and Ricco."

"You work for Baxter Wardell, don't you?" I said. "You're his front man. His man in San Francisco."

Frazer transferred his fugitive stare to me. When he answered it was in a voice that had suddenly gone dead. "I don't know what you mean, Lieutenant. But—" He plucked at the robe, drawing it across his pudgy thighs. "But I've got to get dressed. I'm sorry, but—"

"When Wardell found out that Murdock could send him to prison for what I.P.I. had done—when he found out that Murdock was coming here, to find him—he told you to arrange Murdock's murder." Deliberately, I spoke in a low, resigned monotone, as if Frazer's complicity and subsequent conviction were already an accomplished fact—regrettable, but unavoidable. "You contacted Annunzio, in Miami. You told him to fly to San Francisco. You probably worked through Ricco. You gave Ricco two keys—one to your garage, the other to your car. For a hit man, a car's always a problem. If it's stolen, it's on a hot sheet. If it's his—or if he rents it—he's stuck with it. So your idea made sense. It minimized the risk all around. If the murder went as planned, Annunzio would take your car and pick up Blake, on Polk Street, for his driver. Together, they'd pick up Murdock, who probably thought he was meeting an informant, or maybe one of Wardell's representatives, trying to make a deal—trying to buy him off, maybe. And it went down just like you'd planned it, too—at first. Annunzio killed Murdock, no sweat. Afterward—after they'd dumped the body—Annunzio would've dropped Blake off. Then he would've parked your car somewhere, in a prearranged spot. Everything would've been cool. By midnight Annunzio would've been on a plane. But then there was a traffic accident. So you had to go to a fall-back plan. You reported the car stolen. It was a gamble—a terrible gamble, since you'd already told Simcich the car wasn't stolen. But you didn't have a choice. You had to—"

"No. Jesus Christ, you—you've got it all wrong. You—Christ—you've—" Slowly, doggedly, he began to shake his head. Once more the robe parted across his thighs, this time unheeded. Frazer's eyes were fixed on the center of my chest, staring hard. "You've got it wrong," he repeated dully. "All wrong."

"Then tell me how it happened," I said softly. "This is your chance—your first chance, and your last chance. You're a lawyer. You know how it works. You help us, we help you. Right now we need you. You're the one with the pieces to the puzzle. You've got something to trade. We need you, so you can help yourself. But if you don't cooperate, and somebody else *does* cooperate, you're screwed. We'll come down on you like a ton of bricks, to teach the next guy a lesson. That's how the game goes."

"We know how much money you make, Frazer," Canelli said. "And we know where it comes from. We've got that part all figured out."

As Canelli spoke, Frazer's beard-stubbled face had lost its color. The pulsebeat at his forehead was hammering now. The muscles on his cheek had gone wild. But still he wouldn't speak.

"You're going to spend the night in jail, Frazer," I said. "You're not going to a dinner party. You're going to jail. And Wardell's not going to help—not even from behind the scenes. He's gone. Split. He's left it all to you. Everything."

He blinked. "Gone?" With obvious effort he raised his eyes to meet mine. "Gone?"

"He's gone, and we don't think he'll be back," Canelli lied. "He could be in Mexico by now. Or South America. And he's not coming back. Not until he's off the hook, anyhow."

"Not until he's off the hook, and you're *on* the hook," I said.

"For murder," Canelli said softly. "For murder one. And all because a little old lady in a Mercedes ran a red light."

"No—" Frazer began to shake his head. "No. You—you've got it all wrong."

"Then tell us," I prompted quietly. "Tell us how it went."

"There's—" He closed his eyes. Suddenly his pale, haggard face was glazed with sweat. "There's another man, in New York. He did it all—the whole thing. He made the plans. I just—just did what he told me, that's all."

"Who is he? What's his name?"

"It's—" Again, his eyes closed. Then, speaking in a hoarse whisper: "It's Casanza. John Casanza."

"What plans did he make? When? How?"

"He—he called me about three weeks ago. First Mr. Wardell called and said Casanza would be calling. And then, a few days later, Casanza called."

"Did Wardell tell you to do what Casanza said to do?"

He nodded—a slow, defeated bobbing of his head.

"Answer that question, Mr. Frazer. Don't just nod."

"The—" He licked at his lips. "The answer is—yes." He spoke in a low, toneless voice. With a single word, barely audible, he'd connected Baxter Wardell to murder. For Frazer, it was all over. We were his only hope now.

"What's the rest of it?" I asked. "What happened after that?"

"For a while," he said, "nothing happened. Then, eight days ago, Casanza flew here, to San Francisco. He said that the thing was going critical. That's the way he talks." As he tried to smile, Frazer's lips twisted grotesquely. "He talks like a scientist."

"Describe him," I ordered.

"He's about thirty years old. Maybe thirty-five. He's very—very glib. Very smooth. He's very plausible, too. And very—" Frazer paused, frowning. "Very *viable*. He could've been a Harvard graduate—a corporate officer. Anything. He was very businesslike. He even carried an attaché case. We had a drink at the Carnelian Room. He told me, very concisely, that he was flying a man out from the East Coast to 'put things back in sync,' as he said. He told me to stay close to my phone Monday and Tuesday.

He'd call me, he said, and give me a phone number. I was to take the number, and go to a pay phone, and call him back. Which I did. I was told to put my car key and the key to my garage in an envelope, and leave the envelope with a bartender named Ricco, down in the Tenderlion. My car would be "used" during the next few days. Later, it would be left somewhere, and I'd be told where I could pick it ip." With an effort he looked directly into my eyes. "It—it happened just like you said." He blinked at me. His mouth twitched hopefully, as if we might share a smile. When I didn't respond, he quickly looked away, ashamed of the overture. It was happening to Frazer the way I'd seen it happen to countless others. His life had changed. He was a different man than he'd been just moments before. He was a criminal now, and an object of contempt: a lost, broken man. So we couldn't smile together.

Finally, shaking his head and sighing, he said, "I didn't know it would be Wednesday night. I didn't know it until Simcich came over and told me the car was gone. And then, my God, it suddenly came over me that it was *happening*. Whatever it was, it was *happening*. I—somehow—I didn't think anything would happen. Nothing serious, I mean. I'd deluded myself, you see. Closed my eyes."

"Did you know about Wardell's problems with Murdock? With the FBI?"

"No. Nothing. I swear to God."

"Did you every hear of a man named Simpson?"

"No."

"What's the exact nature of the work you do for Wardell?"

Again, his mouth twitched grotesquely, imitating a smile. With one hand he made a small, wry gesture. "I'm a go-fer, really. I do what he tells me to do—what he pays me to do. He's got a half dozen like me."

"Do you function as a lawyer?"

"Sometimes, but not often. He operates from three

cities—New York, Washington and San Francisco. New York is where the deals are made. Washington is where the strings are pulled. And San Francisco—" He hesitated. "San Francisco's where a lot of people come for money."

"Payoffs, you mean? Under-the-table money?"

He nodded. "If I've got a specialty, I suppose it's laundering money. Then, once it's clean I drive out to the airport and wait. I spend a lot of time at the airport. Sometimes I fly to other airports, and wait. I meet a lot of important people. You'd be surprised."

"I doubt it." I studied him for a moment before I said, "When Casanza said that things were "going critical," what did you think he meant?"

"I thought that Mr. Wardell had a problem that could only be resolved—" He hesitated. "By someone like Casanza."

"What do you mean by that?"

"I mean that Casanza was obviously a—" Again he hesitated, choosing a word: "A thug. A high-level thug."

"Does Wardell use people like Casanza often?"

"No, not often."

"But he does use them."

Frazer nodded. "Sometimes it becomes necessary. Force is a part of life—and business, too. A lot of people don't realize it but it's true. A contract is breached, security is threatened—force is required. It's like countries, using armies. It's the same principle. It's regrettable but necessary. Mr. Wardell is a very rich, very powerful man. He's an—an institution unto himself, like a king. And he makes enemies. So he needs an enforcement arm, just like a king does, or a government. It's that simple."

"Has there ever been a murder before this happened?"

"No. Not that I know anything about. I—" He blinked. "I'd heard of broken legs and arms. But that's all."

"Murder was threatened, though. For an enforcer, death is always the bottom line."

"I don't know anything about death, Lieutenant," he said, speaking in a dull, exhausted voice. "I know about laundering money and making payoffs. But I don't know anything about death or murder. And I didn't know anything about Murdock—or about his murder. I've told you everything I know—everything I do. Mr. Wardell called me, to introduce Casanza. When Casanza came out, I knew that he was an enforcer—that he needed my car to do some kind of dirty job. I knew that someone would be threatened—hurt, maybe. But that's all I knew. It's all I wanted to know. I don't ask questions."

"You knew that it was illegal, though."

"Yes," he answered. "Or at least I suspected. But—" Hopelessly, he shook his head. "But what's legal? What's illegal? Sometimes, when I can't sleep I stare at the ceiling and think that I'm a bagman. I arrange payoffs. But that in itself isn't illegal. It's the intent, I tell myself, that makes it illegal. And as long as I don't know the intent, I'm not guilty of anything. There's nothing wrong, per se, with giving money to people at airports. And there's nothing wrong, per se, with loaning my car to Casanza." He paused, rubbing his hands uncertainly along his bare thighs. "As long as I don't ask questions," he said, "I'm clean."

"That's a trap that a lot of people fall into," Canelli said.

"I'm clean," Frazer repeated, speaking in a dogged, defeated voice. "You'll see."

"If your story's right—if it's provable—then you're probably clean. Or, at least, clean enough. You'll probably get off. But the problem is—" I gestured for him to precede me into the hallway. "The problem is that we have to catch a few of the bad guys before we can prove your story." I watched his weak, ruined face convulse, then said, "I'll leave Inspector Canelli here with you. He'll take you downtown."

188

Twenty

I drove to a nearby restaurant and used a pay phone to call Friedman, at headquarters. His private line was busy. I called the operator, ordering her to buzz Friedman through the switchboard. Trying to keep the excitement out of my voice, careful not to use names on the switchboard line, I recounted the Frazer interrogation. When I'd finished, my reward was a long, low whistle.

"If he'll put his name to that," Friedman said, "we've got a big fish in the net."

"And a chance at a lot bigger fish."

"The man with the P-51." He sounded somber—chastened, almost. I could guess the reason. The prospect of arresting Baxter Wardell for murder was awesome. Friedman was imagining himself leaving the City Club with Wardell in custody.

"Speaking of the P-51, what'd the FAA say?"

"He hasn't filed a flight plan. Either he was conning us, or he changed his plans. Or both."

"Did you get directions to the airstrip?"

"I got them," he answered. "But I don't think you should use them."

"Why not?"

"Several reasons. First, you're not supposed to go after Big Fish without permission. Second—" I could imagine him with two fingers raised. "Second, if you tell him what you just told me, you've got to be prepared to take him into custody. Which you're not. Which means that he can run."

"If he runs, it's an admission of guilt."

"Running is running."

"I don't agree with you. If I tell him what I told you—and if he runs—we've got a case."

"But no suspect in handcuffs."

"Come on, Pete. Use your head. Someone like that doesn't disappear. He can't. It would be like trying to hide the *Enterprise*."

"He can fly down to, say, Costa Rica. He can buy the country and live in it like a hotel. It's been done, you know."

"Did you ever stop to think that if he did that, Dwyer might have his cake while he's eating it?"

"Let's go back to my first point," he said. "You'd not only be acting without permission, you'd be acting against orders. Specific orders."

I was ready for him: "My orders are to find Barbara Murdock, and talk to her. I think I know where she is. I've got an independent party to confirm it—Babcock. So I'm going to find her. I'm following orders."

"Don't forget Annunzio. He's still loose, you know."

"Where was he reported last? Be honest."

"At the San José airport," he admitted. But, stubbornly, he came back to the attack: "I've got another objection."

"What is it?"

"There's something strange about this Marin County junket of Barbara's. It sounds wrong. It doesn't add up."

"It adds up to me. She's probably been trying to corner Big Fish. Maybe she's succeeded. She found out where he's gone, and she's going to confront him."

"Nobody corners him unless he wants to be cornered. Which is precisely why it all sounds wrong."

"Where is the airstrip, anyhow?"

"It's almost due west of Novato."

"That's not far. It's an hour's drive."

"I still don't like it."

"Trust me." Secretly, I smiled. Whenever he tried to entice me into the cat-and-mouse games he was constantly playing with Dwyer, or the FBI, or assorted politicians, Friedman airily advised me to trust him.

I heard him sigh—heard papers rustle. Reluctantly, he gave me directions to the airstrip.

"That's out of your jurisdiction, you know," he said. "Spit on the sidewalk in Marin County, and you're screwed."

"Trust me," I repeated. I couldn't resist saying it.

"Want me to go with you?"

"No. Wait for Canelli and Big Fish's friend. Get a signed statement. Right now, nothing's more important than that."

"Big deal."

I switched on the dome light and spread the Marin County map on the seat beside me. Driving on freeways, I'd made the thirty-five miles from San Francisco to Novato in less than an hour. But the next five miles had taken almost a half hour. Following Friedman's directions, I'd left the freeway and driven west through the sprawling tracts of flat-top suburban houses that surrounded Novato. I'd continued west on a two-lane county road that led into the foothills of the low mountain range that paralleled the coast at a distance of perhaps ten miles. As the road became narrower and steeper, winding its way precariously up the side of a small mountain, the surface of the road changed from concrete to cracked asphalt, and finally to rough, rutted gravel. According to Friedman, Wardell's airstrip was located on a plateau that ran along the top of the mountain range. The entire distance from the freeway to the airstrip, again according to Friedman, was eight miles and six-tenths. I'd already come almost seven miles.

I switched off the dome light. In the glare of my headlights I saw thick-growing trees and brush crowding both sides of the road. It seemed impossible that Baxter Wardell would live in this rugged, rustic terrain, or that he would subject himself to this bone-jolting ride. Had I made a wrong turn? Misinterpreted Friedman's directions? For the third time in the last mile, I switched on the radio and tried to contact San Francisco Communications, almost forty miles away. As before, I could hear only static.

Realizing that I had no choice but to go forward, at least until I found a place wide enough to turn around, I put the drive lever in "low" and resumed the slow, twisting climb. As the grade increased, the engine began to labor, running rough. I glanced at the temperature gauge and saw the needle almost touching the red. The rear wheels were spraying gravel, clawing for traction. Ahead, the road turned sharply to the right. Reluctant to lose speed on the steep grade, I swung into the turn as fast as I dared and slammed on the brakes when a swift, brown shape flashed in the headlight's beams. It was a deer, dashing into the trees—gone. Swearing, I moved my foot from the brake to the accelerator, resuming the car-killing climb. Fighting the car into the next turn, I glanced in the mirror. I saw a dark shape on the road behind me. Was it metallic—a car? Or was it an animal? When I'd first turned west on the county road, I'd seen lights in my mirror. Thinking of Annunzio, I'd pulled to the side and let the car pass. A half mile farther along, the car had turned into a private road. Since then, I'd seen nothing behind me—until now. Easing off on the gas, I kept my eyes on the mirror. But the road switched again, and the dark trees blotted out whatever I'd seen.

Could it be Annunzio, following without lights?

Accelerating as fast as I dared into the next blind turn, I clamped on the brakes, turned off the engine and switched off the lights. I twisted in the seat, straining to see back through the darkness behind me.

If someone was following me, he'd either dropped farther behind or else matched my quick maneuver. I rolled down my window, listening for the sound of an engine. Nothing.

Turning again to face front, I drew my revolver, put it on the seat beside me and turned the ignition key—all the while watching the black, blank mirror. The overheated engine whirred, tried to catch—and failed. Had I flooded it? I turned the key again, waited while the engine ground over and over. As I neutralized the key, I caught the unmistakable odor of raw gasoline. The engine was flooded. Cursing—still watching the mirror—I floorboarded the accelerator, left my foot clamped down and turned the key. It was a last, desperate effort. If the engine didn't catch, I'd be forced to sit in the darkness until the carburetor dried out. The engine whirred, labored and began to grind down. The battery was failing. But then, small miracle, I heard a quickening, a hiccupped explosion—and finally a damp, faltering roar as the engine caught. When the engine's note deepened, I cautiously lifted my foot, then put the transmission in low. I wouldn't stop again until I'd reached the crest of the mountain.

Until the final tenth of a mile I was certain I'd taken a wrong turn—that I would be forced to return to the freeway and try again. But suddenly the road leveled and began to widen. I felt the tires running smoothly on asphalt, not bumping over gravel. Another hundred yards brought me to a huge gate suspended between two massive, brick pillars. A "W" was worked into the wrought iron of the gate. A small Japanese car was parked a short distance away, just at the edge of my headlight's swath.

Letting the engine run, I switched off the headlights and once more twisted in the seat, scanning the road behind. I let a full minute elapse—sixty long, slow counts. The darkened tree-shapes were undisturbed, revealing nothing. The only light I could see came from far down in the valley below: a single pinprick in the night. I glanced at my watch. The time was ten minutes after seven. I wondered whether the moon would rise tonight. If I were a county sheriff, I'd know the answer.

Finally I turned in the seat to stare at the gate. Without doubt it was electrically controlled. As my eyes became accustomed to the darkness I could make out the blacktop roadway extending beyond the gate and disappearing over a low rise. Friedman had said that in addition to the airstrip, there was a house, a caretaker's cottage, a hangar for the P-51 and a two-car garage—all hidden, apparently, beyond the rise, invisible in the darkness that suddenly seemed to surround me like the inside of some vast black dome.

Suddenly the noise of the car's engine sounded too loud—too risky, somehow. Pulling into a parking space beside the car, a Datsun, I raced my engine to clear the carburetor, then turned the switch off and pocketed the keys. With the engine off, the silence was complete: oppressive, palpable, dangerous. Then, through the open window I began to hear the noises of the night: crickets, and frogs, and other sounds less specific. I reached below the dash and switched on the police radio. This time, through the static, I could hear faint, garbled voices: bored-sounding dispatchers, and laconic officers, answering. My position on top of the mountain had helped—but not enough. I knew that I couldn't contact Communications.

I holstered my revolver, took a flashlight from the glove compartment, locked my car and walked to the Datsun. The driver's door was locked, but the passenger's door was open. Playing around the car's interior, the beam of my

194

flashlight revealed nothing. Except for a single map stamped Budget-Rent-A-Car, the glove compartment was empty. Backing out of the car, I was about to close the door when I saw a bit of folded paper protruding from between the right front seat and the control console. The paper unfolded into a sheet of Beresford Hotel stationery, with directions to the Wardell retreat written in a bold, strong script.

Barbara Murdock had gotten there first.

I dropped the directions on the front seat, closed the Datsun's door and stood beside the car, listening. Except for the close by chirping of insects and the distant wail of a coyote, the night around me was silent—ominously silent. From the eastern sky, far away, I heard the rolling whisper of a jetliner. It was a faint sound—but loud enough, perhaps, to mask the idling of an engine on the road behind me. So, for another long minute I stood motionless, listening intently for some alien sound. All I could hear were the insects and the animals.

I turned to the gate and tentatively pushed at it, unsuccessfully. A button was set in the center of the square locking device that secured the two halves of the gate. I pressed the button, heard a click, and felt the gate move. The electronic lock had been set to open.

Holding the flashlight unlit in my hand, I walked along the blacktop driveway that led to the top of the rise, a hundred feet beyond the gate. The night was clear; the sky was filled with stars. Even without a moon I could make out the rough outlines of the surrounding terrain. The driveway was about twenty-five feet wide, bordered on each side by low-growing hedges. Behind me, the gate joined a six-foot cyclone fence that probably surrounded the property. For the first time I saw a pair of floodlights that topped each of the two brick pillars. The spotlights and the gate's lock were doubtless tied into an overall electronic security surveillance system.

But why were the floodlights unlit? Why was the lock set to open when the button was pushed?

And why was there no sign of Barbara Murdock—no sign of life?

As I came closer to the rise, I moved instinctively to my right, away from the center of the driveway and into the shadow of a huge pine tree. Standing beside the tree, I was looking down on Wardell's mountaintop domain: a long, pale ribbon of concrete runway flanked on the near side by the buildings Friedman had described: a hangar; a long, rambling house built along the crest of the plateau and two smaller buildings. The driveway curved toward the house, where it divided in two, one branch leading to the tarmac, the other to a carport attached to the house.

The place was deserted. The hangar was closed, the house and the two buildings were dark. Slowly, responding to some deep, primitive urge to move silently and cautiously, I began walking down the curving slope of the driveway. Here, there was no cover—no sheltering trees, not even a hedge. The driveway had been scraped out of the rock and shale native to the barren, wind-scoured mountaintop.

I'd almost reached the carport when I saw a faint gleam of light from inside the house. I was standing inside the empty carport now, concealed in deep shadow. I stepped to a small window and looked inside the house. The light came from a hallway, and probably originated in a room that opened off the hall—a bedroom, or a bathroom. Without doubt, the light had been left to discourage prowlers. On top of a mountain range, it seemed a futile measure, strangely citified.

From the window I moved to a door that connected the carport to the house. The door was locked. I walked from the carport to the edge of the concrete ribbon of the runway: a long, ghostly white path in the starlight.

What did they mean, these strangely deserted buildings, and the abandoned Datsun?

If Barbara Murdock had been here, where had she gone?

Had Baxter Wardell been here and left, flying in his P-51 to Los Angeles?

There was one way to find out.

Walking quickly now, irrationally in a hurry and no longer wary of discovery, I walked down the runway to the hangar. A small access door was set in the hangar's huge folding aluminum doors. The access door was locked. I rattled the flimsy door and felt it yield. Switching on the flashlight, I examined the lock. It was minimal, easily slipped. I took a plastic credit card from my pocket, probed, pushed and finally felt the door swing open. Following the flashlight's unsteady beam, I stepped into the pungent, oily-smelling hangar to face the shape of a low-winged airplane, the P-51.

If Wardell had flown to Los Angeles, it hadn't been in his fighter plane.

Faint light from a row of skylights fell across a workbench set against the hangar's far wall. Outside, I'd seen three wires strung to the hangar: two for electricity, probably one for a phone. As I moved toward the workbench, I heard a sound from the direction of the airplane. It was a soft scraping—unmistakably a shoe moving furtively on concrete.

I switched off the flashlight, drew my gun and dropped to a crouch. "All right. Come out of there. Come toward me, slow and easy. This is a gun. And it's pointed right at you."

I heard a gasp, then a muffled sob.

A woman.

"Barbara? Is that you?"

No response. No sound. Could she have a gun?

"It's Hastings. Lieutenant Hastings."

"Oh, my God." It was a low, desperate moan. "Jesus God. Lieutenant."

"Come here."

A dim figure separated itself from the shape of the airplane. She ducked beneath the engine cowling and came slowly, hesitantly toward me. As she moved across the oblong of uncertain light that fell through the doorway, I saw that she wore slacks and a heavy sweater. Switching on my flashlight, I asked, "Where's the light switch?"

"I don't know." I could hear a tremor of fear in her voice. She was standing close beside me—as a child might stand, mutely seeking comfort from a grownup.

"What're you doing here, anyhow?" As I spoke, I angrily holstered my revolver. "You're—Christ—you're causing a lot of people a lot of trouble."

"I was supposed to meet Wardell. Baxter Wardell."

"Is he here? Did you see him?"

"No. Nobody's here. Just—" I could hear her swallow. "Just me."

"Is Wardell going to come?"

"I—I don't know. I called him—told him I wanted to talk with him. He said he'd meet me here."

"When did you talk to him?"

"About noon. In San Francisco."

"When were you supposed to meet him? What time?"

"About a half hour ago. Seven, he said. Between seven and seven-thirty."

"Have you been here since then? Since seven?"

"Yes."

"Was the gate open when you got here? On the latch?"

"Yes. I pushed the button, and it opened. Wardell told me it would."

"What're you doing here? In the hangar?"

"It was the only place I could get into. I—" I heard her voice falter. "I wanted to be inside."

"Was the hangar door unlocked?"

"Yes. I—I locked it. Then I heard you."

"You should've stayed in your car. This is silly, what

you're doing. It could be dangerous. There could be guard dogs. Anything." I felt a surge of irrational anger. She could have endangered me, along with herself. It always happened, when civilians meddled in police business. "Come on—" I pocketed my flashlight and took her arm. "We're leaving. I'll follow you down the hill."

"But what about Wardell?"

"He's not here and he's not coming. He's supposed to be on his way to Los Angeles." I spoke impatiently, harshly. "There's something wrong with this," I said. "Can't you see that? Can't you *feel* it? This place shouldn't be deserted, or dark. And the gate shouldn't be open. It's a setup."

"A setup?"

"Never mind." Still holding her arm, I turned her toward the door. "Let's go."

Unresisting, she walked with me to the door, then out on the tarmac. During the time we'd been inside the hangar, a moon had come up. It was a three-quarter moon, still partially obscured by the distant horizon and by the pine trees that bordered Wardell's property on the east. I pulled the door closed behind us, made sure the lock had latched, then caught up with Barbara, walking ahead. She walked with long, firm strides—a hiker's gait, strong and purposeful. To myself, I smiled. She'd recovered her assurance. A few moments before, close beside me in the darkened hangar, she'd been a different, softer woman.

"That airplane," she said. "What is it?"

"A P-51. A World War Two fighter."

"Does Wardell fly it?"

"Yes."

Clearing the corner of the hangar, we turned together into the curving driveway that led up the slope toward the gate. Almost at the crest of the slope, I had momentarily turned to look back over my shoulder at the hangar when I felt Barbara's hand on my arm.

199

"Lieutenant. Look."

Following her gesture, I saw the shape of a car without lights. It was moving with slow, menacing purpose, coming directly toward us. Blocking both my car and the Datsun, it stopped just short of the gate.

"Don't move," I whispered. "Freeze."

"Who is it?" she breathed.

"I don't know. But it could be trouble. If we don't move, he might not see us."

We were standing in the center of the wide driveway. The carport was about fifty feet to our right; the hangar was fifty feet to our left. We'd been caught in the open, on a bare, rocky slope. Every moment the light of the rising moon came brighter through the pine trees.

Had he seen us? Could he—

Headlights suddenly blazed, blinding us.

"Quick. *Run.*" I turned her roughly toward the hangar. "Dodge. *Run.*" Bending double, I was pounding down the sloping asphalt, slipping once, almost falling. Behind me, I heard a low, desperate gasp. Turning as I ran, I saw Barbara fall. But quickly, she rolled, scrambled to her feet—a sure-footed, gutsy lady. I broke stride, momentarily turning to confront the terrible glare of the headlights, instinctively protecting her. Then, together, we ran around the corner of the hangar—safe.

For a moment, one single moment, safe.

Gesturing her back against the hangar wall, I peered cautiously around the corner. Because of the slope, I couldn't see the gate or the cars. I could only see the twin headlight beams, angled up into the sky. The lights hadn't moved; the car was motionless.

If the car belonged on the property, an electronic opener would have swung open the gate. By now the car would be coming down the driveway, headed for either the house or the hangar. So the car was strange to the property—a visitor, or an intruder.

Or an executioner.

From where we stood, the glare of the canted headlights had deepened the shadow, tempting me to dart from the hangar to the house. I could circle the house, and come at him from an unsuspected direction, surprising him.

But I couldn't take the woman with me. And I couldn't leave her, either.

So we must wait. We must—

Suddenly the lights shifted; something had deflected the symmetry of the two yellow beams. Now a head was silhouetted in the glare—then shoulders—then a torso—finally the full figure of a man. He stood at the top of the rise, motionless. Seen from below, he was unnaturally tall and menacing. His legs were braced. His left hand hung empty at his side.

His right hand held the unmistakable shape of a gun— a big, bulky gun. A machine pistol, or a submachine gun.

"Jesus," I breathed.

"What is it?" Barbara whispered. She couldn't see the figure. But she'd seen the headlight beams shift in the darkness.

"Whoever he is, he's got a gun."

"A watchman?"

"I'm not sure. But we're targets out here. Easy targets. We're not taking any chances." I strode swiftly to the hangar's small access door. Facing the door, I balanced myself, foot raised, ready to smash the lock.

But I shouldn't—couldn't. The lock would protect us.

I handed Barbara the flashlight, told her to shine it on the lock, and took out the credit card. Working at the lock, my fingers felt thick and awkward, made clumsy with haste and apprehension. Glancing over my shoulder as I worked at the lock, I saw darkness suddenly return to the void beyond the hangar. Whoever was out there, he'd switched off his headlights.

The lock yielded. The door came open. Quickly, we slipped inside the hangar.

"Close the door," I said. "Lock it. See if you can brace something against it." As I spoke, I threw my flashlight beam in a circle around us. I saw a row of shoulder-height windows set in the rear wall. If I turned on the lights inside the hangar, we would be easy targets for someone shooting through the windows.

And by now the driver of the car could have reached the hangar.

I dodged under the P-51's silvery wing, making for the workbench. At the far end of the bench, on the wall, I saw a phone. I clicked off the flashlight, lifted the receiver and dialed the operator.

"This is a police emergency," I said, and gave her the number of the San Francisco Communications. Moments later I was talking to Friedman. Hearing the familiar voice, I felt a sudden rush of stomach-empty, knee-trembling relief.

"I'm at Wardell's place," I said, speaking in a harsh, hoarse whisper, cupping my hand around the receiver. "Barbara Murdock's here. We're alone. All alone, in the hangar. The place is deserted. It feels like a setup. And just a minute ago someone came in a car. He's got a gun. It looks like a Uzi. I want you to call the Highway Patrol. Tell them to get a car up here. Fast. Tell them to hit the siren. Hard."

"Are you sure it's a Uzi?"

"I'm not sure of anything."

"Be careful," he said. "Don't be a hero."

"I won't." I replaced the phone on its hook and picked up the flashlight. With my revolver in my hand, I made my way slowly along the workbench. Ahead, the P-51's wing tip overhung the bench. With the moonlight coming through the overhead skylights, the interior of the hangar was brighter now. As I stooped to go under the airplane's wing, I saw Barbara struggling with a wooden packing case, dragging it along the floor toward the door. Silently, I moved to help her. Weighing about a hundred pounds, the box was less than three feet tall. It might deter someone coming through the door, but it wouldn't stop him. As we jammed the box against the door I looked back toward the rear wall, with its row of windows. If I could see through the windows, the intruder could see me, too.

"Here—" I pulled her around the fighter's huge four-bladed propeller, and back under the engine. In that position, the plane's fuselage and wings would protect her from fire through the windows.

"Crouch down here," I said. "Keep your head below the level of the wings."

Dropping to one knee beside me, she whispered, "What's a Uzi?"

"It's a machine pistol," I said. "And it's illegal. A watchman wouldn't have one."

"Would a policeman have one?"

I looked at her. "Yes," I answered, "a policeman could have one. But—"

From the direction of the access door, I heard a click, then the indistinct scraping of metal on metal. Someone was trying the door. As I listened to the soft, furtive sound, I was remembering Barbara's directions, written on Beresford stationery. I'd left the directions on the seat of the Datsun, unfolded, in plain view. If the intruder was Annunzio, looking for Barbara, I'd given him all he needed.

Yet, if he'd looked inside the Datsun, he would also have looked inside my car. He would have seen the police radio. He'd know he faced a policeman—with a gun.

Then I remembered Blake, shot as he talked to me.

If it was Annunzio, a policeman wouldn't deter him. With an Uzi, he could kill us both in a single burst.

I touched Barbara's arm, whispered in her ear, "He's at the door. Quick. Get behind the airplane. Get it between you and the door. Never mind the windows. Stay down. Flat on the floor."

"But—"

"*Do* it." I shoved her away from me, then crouched low behind the airplane's wingroot. Spreading my feet wide on the floor, I flattened myself on the wing, my cocked revolver trained on the door. If he forced the lock, the door would only open an inch before it struck the heavy packing case. In that instant I could fire through the lightweight aluminum door. Unless he were crouched below the level of the case, I could—

Machinegun fire shattered the silence. Above Barbara's scream, I heard the savage whine of ricocheting bullets, felt the high velocity slugs tearing into the aluminum skin of the airplane.

He'd shot away the lock. The door moved, then struck the packing case. Aiming just above the dark oblong shape of the case, I fired.

"I'm a policeman," I shouted. "Give it up."

Another burst tore through the door, rattling on the airplane like hailstones from hell. I fired another shot. I carried five rounds in my revolver. Three live rounds remained. Until I could see a target, I couldn't risk firing again.

How many rounds did the Uzi's clip carry? Twenty? Twenty-five? How many spare clips did he have? Two? Three?

I looked over my shoulder, back toward the row of shoulder-height windows.

He could only be in one place at a time—either at the door or the windows. If I kept my head—didn't panic—I could keep the airplane between us, moving as he moved. Until help arrived, I must go on the defensive.

Scraping on the concrete floor, the box was moving. An inch. Two inches. Six inches. Crouched down behind the box, using it as a shield, he was coming through the door.

I pushed myself away from the wing and ran on tiptoe back toward the airplane's tail assembly, where Barbara crouched.

"Get back to the windows," I hissed. "*Quick*." Beside the workbench, I'd seen a folded stepladder. Pocketing my flashlight and holstering my revolver, I lifted the ladder and ran with it toward the rear of the hangar. Behind me the crate was grating across the concrete. Any moment, he would have room to squeeze through. At the windows now, I swung the ladder at the nearest pane, turning my head away from stinging splinters of flying glass. I propped the ladder against the wall, its top resting on the window sill. Barbara was close behind me.

"Get out," I whispered. "Go to the cars and wait for the Highway Patrol. When they come, tell them what's happened. *Hurry*."

As she put her foot on the ladder, I moved to my left, toward the workbench. Had he slipped inside the hangar while I was at the rear windows? Squatting on my heels beneath the airplane's wing, I saw the aluminum door slowly opening. I watched it swing inward until it touched the packing crate. The door cleared the frame by a foot, room enough for him to slip through. I rose from my crouch, drew my revolver and darted behind the end of the workbench. Now, when he came through the door, the advantage would be mine. He would be exposed. I would be protected. With the revolver cocked. I raised myself cautiously behind the bench, risking only my head and shoulders. I held the revolver in my right hand. With my left hand I reached inside my jacket and unclipped the band of ten extra cartridges I carried on my belt. With my eyes fixed on the door, I fumbled awkwardly with the cartridges, slipping them from their leather loops and fanning them on the bench. In the silence I heard glass falling. Barbara was climbing through the window. She—

Quickly he came through the doorway, moving in a low, elusive crouch. I saw him drop to one knee and turn the gun toward the rear windows, taking aim. Bright blossoms of fire twinkled from the Uzi's muzzle as I steadied my revolver on his torso, corrected, squeezed the trigger. The sound of my single shot was lost in the machine gun's ear-bursting clatter. Behind me, glass was crashing. Barbara was screaming.

In front of me, the Uzi's muzzle still sparkled, dancing delicately in the darkness as the barrel turned toward me. The wooden workbench shuddered, taking the bullets. I cocked my revolver—and squeezed the trigger. Kicking up, the revolver barrel momentarily obscured his twinkling machine gun, his torso, the shape of his head.

One shot remained for me. Just one, before I must reload.

Suddenly there was silence, still echoing to the sound of gunfire. A thousand bits of glass were tinkling musically, striking the concrete floor of the hangar.

In front of me, the shadow of a man was crouched close to the floor. Over the sights of my revolver I saw the figure braced on all fours, head hanging, rocking more precariously now. I heard him cough once, sigh gently—and fall heavily to the concrete.

I straightened to my full height, ducked beneath the P-51's wing and moved cautiously toward him, my gun trained on his head. He'd fallen on his side, with face away from me. The butt of the machine pistol protruded from beneath his torso. I pulled at the Uzi until it came free. I holstered my revolver and laid the Uzi carefully on the workbench, with its muzzle pointed to the wall. Later, I would disarm it.

I turned toward the row of shattered windows.

"Barbara?"

No response. When he'd fired the first burst, I'd heard her scream—then heard nothing.

With my feet crackling on the broken glass, I walked to the ladder. I'd last seen her with her foot on the first step, climbing. During the time it had taken him to enter the hangar, she could have reached the window sill. But if his burst had been accurate, she—

From behind me I heard the sound of metal lightly striking wood. It was the access door, striking the packing case. Turning sharply, I saw the shape of a head breaking the rectangle of the door.

"Barbara?"

"Yes. Oh—" Her voice caught. "Oh, yes. Are you all right?"

"I'm all right." I'd been standing on the first step of the ladder. As I moved heavily toward her, I took out my flashlight and used it to find a light switch, located at the far end of the workbench. The cold glow of fluorescent lights fell on the body lying close beside the hangar doors. I circled the boneless, amorphous pile of clothing with hands and feet and a head attached. Even before I squatted to stare into his empty eyes, I knew he was dead.

"Who is he?" she whispered.

"A killer named Joey Annunzio," I answered. I rose and leaned against the hangar door. Trembling violently, my legs wouldn't support me. My arms were useless. My head was suddenly as heavy as a baby's. It was, I knew, the inevitable backwash of mortal fear: the shameful, secret spasm that always overtook me, afterward.

In the distance, I heard the faint sound of a faraway siren.

"We're lucky," I whispered. "We're very lucky."

Twenty-one

The rain that had been threatening the city for most of the week had finally come. Standing side by side before a rain-streaked window of United's Concourse "A," Barbara Murdock and I watched silently as a half-dozen figures in hooded yellow raincoats loaded a 707 cargo liner. Overhead, the sky was a darkening, lowering gray. Dusk was falling fast. In the fading light, the airport runways glistened like intersecting canals. In the center of the field, a 747 was taking off. As its wheels left the rain-glazed runway, its engines threw up enormous plumes of white spray. With a ganglion of wheels dangling awkwardly beneath its fuselage, the 747 seemed to hesitate in midair, collecting itself for the final effort necessary to leave the ground behind. Then the wheels began to retract. The airliner gained speed as its nose angled upward at a sharper angle. Moments later the 747 disappeared in the dark clouds that overhung the airport.

Beside me, I sensed Barbara stiffening. She was staring down at the tarmac. A fork-lift truck with "United" painted on its side was emerging from the air-cargo hangar. The fork-lift's twin tines held a plain wooden casket.

As the truck approached the open hatch of the cargo plane, the casket was slowly raised to the level of the hatch. I heard Barbara catch her breath. I knew why. She was imagining the coffin tipping on the tines, falling to the tarmac and splitting open.

A moment later the casket disappeared inside the 707. The fork-lift truck backed away, pivoted smartly and lowered its tines as it moved back toward the hangar for another load. I waited for Barbara to turn away from the window, then I fell into step beside her. We began walking slowly down the concourse to United's Gate 8.

"How soon does your plane leave?" I asked.

"Thirty-five minutes."

I pointed to a coffee-and-doughnut counter. "Can I buy you a cup of coffee?"

"No, thanks. I don't drink coffee after four o'clock."

Silently, Barbara walked to a row of plastic chairs and sat down, crossing her legs. She moved with the same calm, controlled precision that I'd first admired when she'd come to my office on Thursday, beginning her ordeal. She wore the same clothing: a leather jacket, twill slacks and an orange scarf knotted at her throat. Since Thursday, neither her appearance nor her manner had changed.

But I could see a change in her eyes. Four days of shock and anger and sorrow and, finally, terror had left a shadow deep behind her handsome brown eyes. I knew that shadow. I knew its origins; I knew the damage it did. I knew how to watch for it and how to measure it. I'd learned how it could sometimes be turned to my advantage.

"If you'd like to," she said, "you can come to the memorial service. It'll probably be Wednesday." She spoke very softly. She didn't look at me as she spoke.

"Thanks, but I doubt whether I could get away."

She let a moment pass before she said, "I'd like to have you come."

"I know that."

And I knew why she wanted me with her at the service. As death connected her finally to her father, death had also connected her to me. Together we'd almost died.

"I haven't thanked you," she said. "I haven't thanked you for anything."

I smiled at her. "There's nothing to thank me for. Besides, you told me where to find the notes. They were the key."

"You saved my life."

Still smiling, I said, "I also saved *my* life."

Gravely, she returned my smile. Then she reached out to touch my arm, just below the shoulder. It was a gesture both simple and complex, signaling both sadness and hope, both courage and fear. But most of all it signaled a lost, desperate longing—a yearning for someone she didn't have, and might never have.

As her hand lingered on my arm, she tried to smile—and failed.

"It's all so—" She blinked against sudden tears, shook her head, bit her lip. Her hand ran down my arm, hesitated, finally fell away. I didn't touch her in return.

"It's all so—so goddamn pointless," she said. "His whole life was pointless, and so was his death. It wasn't even tragic. That would count for something, at least—make a splash. But it wasn't a tragedy. It was all just a waste. A sad, pointless waste," For a moment she paused, still blinking against the tears. Then: "He never liked who he was or where he was. Not really. He was born in Chillicothe. He had a hometown that sounded like a hometown should sound—like picnics, and parades, and senior proms. But he always wanted to—to *be* someone. So he was always ashamed of Chillicothe. So he went to Washington—and finally *was* someone. But Washington is nobody's hometown. I should know. I was born there. It's a place for winners only—a place to stay until your luck changes or your money runs out or your party loses an election. And then you leave. If you don't leave voluntarily, you're asked to leave—in a thousand small, subtle, brutal ways.

"So when his luck ran out and nobody returned his calls, he left town. And finally he came to Los Angeles—another town that's nobody's hometown. This—" Slowly, hopelessly, she shook her head. Her cheeks were wet. "This is a savage country," she said finally. "America is a place where you can't win, even if you're a winner. Because the winners always want more. That's how they get to be winners. And so they're never happy. And unhappy people can turn into savages. They—"

A woman's voice was announcing United Flight 603 to Los Angeles. The voice was low and throaty, a seductive-sounding voice. Barbara turned to look toward the loudspeaker. Then, slowly, she turned back to me. For a moment she looked me full in the face.

"That's my flight."

"Yes." I waited for her to rise, then rose to stand beside her. Slowly, gravely, she extended her hand.

"You're a kind man, Lieutenant. I like you. And I admire you, too."

"Thank you."

"Can I ask you a question? One last question?"

"You can ask. But I'm not sure I can answer. Especially if it's about Baxter Wardell."

"He's in South America, isn't he?"

Holding her gaze, I said, "That's a question I can't answer. And you know it."

But I knew she could see it in my eyes: that, yes, Wardell was gone. I meant for her to see it.

Releasing my hand, she wiped at her tears, digging her knuckles hard into her eyes. It was the dogged, determined gesture of a child who won't be beaten. Finally she said, "It's good that you won't be coming to the memorial service, I guess. Because just now—just this minute—I decided that I'm going to use my father's funeral to tell the truth about why he died, and who ordered him killed. That's the only way his death will mean anything. There'll be a hundred reporters there. And I'm going to tell them." She tried to smile. "It's something that Dad would have approved of—media hype."

I returned her smile. "I'm glad it's Wardell you're out to get this time—not the San Francisco Police Department."

For a moment she didn't reply. Then, suddenly, she came close, gripped my shoulders and kissed me on the mouth, hard.

"Goodbye, Lieutenant," she whispered. "I'll remember you."

She turned and walked toward the boarding gate. Her shoulders were squared, her strides long and straight. She went through the gate without looking back.

About the Author

COLLIN WILCOX was born in Detroit and educated at Antioch College. He's been a San Franciscan since 1950 and lives in a Victorian house that he is "constantly remodeling, with the help of two strong sons." A national director and ex-regional vice president of the Mystery Writers of America, Mr. Wilcox writes "a little more than one book a year."